the Wish List ③

Halfway to Happily Ever After

the Wish List

1 The Worst Fairy Godmother Ever!

2 Keep Calm and Sparkle On!

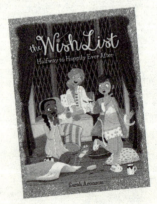

3 Halfway to Happily Ever After

the Wish List 3

Halfway to Happily Ever After

By Sarah Aronson

Scholastic Press

New York

Library of Congress Cataloging-in-Publication Data available

ISBN 978-0-545-94162-4

10 9 8 7 6 5 4 3 2 1   18 19 20 21 22

Printed in the U.S.A.   23

First edition, June 2018

Book design by Maeve Norton

For my sisters, Miriam and Annie

Chapter One

The Vacation That Wasn't

Dear Isabelle,
Please come to my office immediately. It's time to get to
work. We have no time to lose!
—Grandmomma

There was nothing at all to be nervous about.

As Isabelle walked down the long, winding hall from her
bedroom to Grandmomma's large, red office door, she
couldn't decide if she was excited or squeamish, or

something closer to terrified. In theory, studying with Grandmomma (for her entire vacation) was the opportunity of a lifetime. But in real life, it felt more like a punishment. Grandmomma (with the emphasis on *grand*) wasn't helping her for kicks.

She was helping her because she had no choice.

In other words, there was everything to be nervous about.

After two levels of training, Isabelle still hadn't read the *Official Rule Book for Fairy Godmothers*. She daydreamed all the time. Forget the fine print! At the end of Level One, she left Nora, her practice princess (and technically, a regular girl), a jar full of stolen sparkles—just in case she needed a friend—even though this was strictly against the rules.

In Level Two, things only got worse. Isabelle annoyed everyone—especially the two best trainees in the class, Angelica and Fawn. She struggled with her assignment. Helping out Samantha instead of Nora was incredibly difficult—especially when they were in the middle of an epic misunderstanding. Also: Isabelle had a case of the guilts, since Grandmomma had left training to track down missing sparkles!

In the end (as it always does in these types of stories), happily ever after won the day. Samantha and Nora made up. Angelica, Fawn, and Isabelle vowed to be friends, too. Grandmomma returned the missing sparkles, and they had nothing to do with Isabelle's. (She found those sparkles *lickety-split*.) Best of all, after the Extravaganza, Isabelle found a yellow-and-green ring dangling on one of the girl-goyle's claws. She was 99.9 percent sure Clotilda had left it for her because it belonged to their mother. And that it held very powerful magic. And that because of all those things, she shouldn't lose it or drop it or show it to anyone. Not even Grandmomma.

Maybe especially Grandmomma.

Now, as Isabelle stared at the brass lion door knocker in the middle of Grandmomma's office door, she realized she was still wearing the ring. So instead of knocking, Isabelle slipped it off and tucked it into her pocket.

This turned out to be excellent timing, because at the same moment, the door flew open and Grandmomma stood in the archway with her hands on her hips and her lips pursed.

She did not look happy.

"You're late," Grandmomma said, pointing to a small chair that looked like it was made of splintered wood. "Hurry up and sit down. I don't want to waste another second."

Isabelle didn't want to waste another second either, but the chair was really uncomfortable. It was rickety, too—like it might fall to pieces any moment. Also: Every time she fidgeted even the slightest bit, the thing creaked.

It creaked when she turned her neck to peer into the magic mirror. It creaked when she reached for the edge of the spinning wheel that she wasn't supposed to touch. It creaked when she checked out the newest additions to Grandmomma's collections of crowns, pictures, and other magical accessories, from jewels to jump ropes, and, of course, shoes. There were shelves of them—all sizes and styles! On one end of the top shelf—right next to a lovely pair of pink glittery sneakers—was something new. It looked like a regular apple, but it was missing one bite.

Isabelle stood up to get a closer look. "Is that . . ."

"It is." Grandmomma grabbed the shiny red apple and dangled it in front of Isabelle's eyes. "Would you like to touch it? You can, if you hold it by the stem."

Isabelle read the warning label. *Whatever you do, please don't eat.*

It was *that* apple—no doubt about it. "It's so beautiful," she said, marveling at the shine, the color, the perfectly even bite marks. "Does it still work? Where did you find it?"

"In the basement. Just sitting there next to an old measuring cup."

Creak! Isabelle had long since stopped asking for permission to enter the basement. To make sure she didn't sneak in, Grandmomma kept the door locked at all times. She also used magic. (She was not taking any chances.)

That was annoying because, of course, Clotilda had the key. She'd told Isabelle (many times—usually when the lights were out) that in the basement, Grandmomma experimented with sparkles. She neutralized potions and buried mistakes for good. She kept magical tools that had gone out of style. According to Clotilda, Grandmomma and Luciana practiced their most difficult magic in the wee hours of the night—but Isabelle was pretty sure that her sister was just trying to scare her.

By accident, Isabelle touched the core of the apple. She dropped it on the desk. "What should I do?"

Grandmomma pointed to the back of her office and a small sink with spouts that looked like girlgoyles. "Rinse your hands with soap and hot water—all the way up to the elbows."

When Isabelle returned to her seat, Grandmomma said, "Now open your book. You did bring it, didn't you?"

Isabelle had forgotten her book as well as her wand and her glasses. And probably something else, but she couldn't remember what that was.

It was very embarrassing. But not particularly surprising. Isabelle had a long history of forgetting things.

She said, "Let me go back and get them," but Grandmomma was running out of patience fast. She grabbed her wand, and flicked her wrist. Gold and purple sparkles flew all around the room. When they cleared, Isabelle held a book wrapped in plain brown paper marked *12th Edition*—DRAFT. Her glasses, clean and ready to go, fell right onto her nose. Her wand appeared on the desk. And her hair felt clean, as if someone had washed, dried, and styled it.

Isabelle tried to get comfortable. (She knew when Grandmomma was about to deliver a lecture.)

For this one, Grandmomma stood up. She said, "When you go out into the world, you represent all of us. That means you need more than kindness, gusto, and fortitude. You even need more than laser-beam focus. You must be thinking ahead. You have to look and be ready. First impressions are important—especially when it comes to princesses." She told her to turn to the page marked *Important Facts Every Fairy Godmother Should Know If She Wants to Be Great.*

"It's very well written." (That meant she wrote it herself.)

Grandmomma read, "When you meet your princess, keep in mind that there are usually at least two correct answers to any question or wish. That's because princesses are very complex."

Isabelle almost shouted, "Regular girls are even worse," but Grandmomma had more to say, so Isabelle stopped herself and sat still.

"There are a) sweet princesses, the kind that get in trouble by having difficult relatives or because they live in difficult times in history.

"There are b) spunky princesses, who don't need any help finding trouble. (They get into it all on their own.)

"There are c) princesses with varying degrees of spunky and sweet as well as d) intelligence, e) bravery, f) nerve, and

g) goals, and the only way you can tell where they fall on the continuum is to let them make a few mistakes."

Isabelle couldn't help thinking about Nora and Samantha, the two regular friends she had already made happily ever after in Levels One and Two training. Grandmomma was right. They were both sweet and spunky (as well as talented and kind) in different ratios. Even though they thought they could have made many wishes, in the end, what made them happily ever after (or as Angelica would say, H.E.A.) was friendship.

"But isn't that what I did?"

When Grandmomma shook her head, her earrings rattled. "The reason you are here is that you didn't study. Then you spent too much time dawdling. You practically told them what to wish for. You should never do that—even if you know exactly what will make them happy."

Now Isabelle was even more frustrated. "So all I can do is listen? And wait? Even when they have no idea that fairy godmothers exist?"

That seemed unfair. Also like a big waste of time.

Grandmomma must have thought so, too, because she grabbed a copy of her Wish List. (It was the biggest, fattest book on her shelf.) "For the sake of all that is sparkly, when are you going to learn that the Wish List isn't just some souvenir we give you for kicks? It's the encyclopedia of princesses past, present, and future—which means it's also a great how-to manual." She told Isabelle to study hers tonight (perhaps for the first time). "By looking at how other fairy godmothers made it work, you can strengthen your skills. You won't have to beg your practice princess to make her wish."

Isabelle nodded. "Regular girls, too?" (She wasn't complaining. She really wanted to know.)

Grandmomma nodded. "If you don't believe me, look at the first page of the new rule book. The part highlighted in pink."

Isabelle found the section and began to read. *Just like princesses, regular girls (or girls who are not royal and have not wished for anything from us) also deserve happiness. As fairy godmothers, we can make the world better by granting their wishes, too. For the purposes of ease in this book, the word* princess *will refer to all girls who receive a fairy godmother.*

Isabelle pumped her fist. "It's about time!"

Grandmomma told her the better thing to say was thank you.

Isabelle was about to, but then she noticed an unhighlighted line in the middle of the next page: *As an official fairy godmother, you will have a rainbow of sparkles to work with. It will be your job to come up with the right combination of carefully measured colors to assist your princess and ensure her happiness.* "When can we learn that?"

Grandmomma gripped her wand. (She was growing impatient.) "You will learn all about the science of sparkles in Levels Three and Four. Right now, we have to focus on what you should know already." (That was the reason she didn't highlight it.)

So that's what they did. For the rest of the day and every day after that, Isabelle learned the rules about how to greet princesses (politely) and how to impress princesses (with little bits of magic) and how to listen effectively (quietly and with concentration—no distractions). She also practiced a lot of simple magic—until she could demonstrate it *lickety-split*.

And, no surprise to Grandmomma, the practice paid off. By the end of vacation, Isabelle could make a rotten apricot fresh. She could turn all kinds of accessories into magical charms. And she could even create a momentary weather disturbance.

Grandmomma ate an apricot Isabelle had just transformed. "You've done an excellent job, Isabelle," she said, juice dripping from her chin. "If you don't have any questions, why don't you take off the rest of the day?"

Even though Isabelle had a zillion questions, she ran as fast as she could out the door and down the hall, up to the tower, and to the cozy space between the girlgoyles. She couldn't wait to try out the ring. She had waited a really long time already.

But when she settled into her spot, something didn't feel right. The sky was still blue. The grass was still green. The air still smelled fresh. What was it? Then she figured it out. It was the girlgoyle to her left. Taped to her nose was a triangle-shaped note.

Dear Isabelle,
Please meet me and Irene and MaryEllen outside the
center for a super-secret meeting at midnight. Remember:
It's a secret. In other words: Don't tell anyone.

—M

M was Minerva, her friend and the oldest of the three elderly fairy godmothers sent back to training, also known as the Worsts.

This had to be an important meeting.

Midnight was the magic hour.

Chapter Two

Sister Time

*A*n hour later, Isabelle wished that someone in the fairy godmother world had been smart enough to make the magic hour a little bit earlier. Midnight was still a long time away and already she was exhausted. Every second dragged.

It didn't help that the ring seemed to be a dud.

As far as she could tell, it held no secret compartment— no trick lock or button to push. When she pressed it to her heart and thought of Nora and Samantha or her mother, it didn't grow warm or shoot a single sparkle or even fizzle. For kicks, Isabelle tried attaching it to the end of her wand and whirling it over her head, but that was reckless, so she stopped. Magic or not, she didn't want to lose it. Plus, the girlgoyles couldn't get out of the way. If she accidentally hit them, they might chip or crack.

So Isabelle did the one thing she disliked more than anything else. She sat still and waited. And while she waited, she imagined all the things that made her nervous, like lessons, and Luciana, and seeing Angelica and Fawn for the first time since the Extravaganza. She wondered what Nora, Samantha, and their friends Janet and Mason were doing. For some reason, thinking about them made her heart feel heavy—as if something were wrong.

This was the problem with waiting. It was also the problem with being tired and spending too much time with girlgoyles who couldn't warn Isabelle when her imagination was getting away from her. Because the girlgoyles were made of rock (and couldn't talk or move), they couldn't encourage her. Or even pat her on the back. They couldn't wish her luck when it was time to go inside and put on dark-colored clothes and a pair of sunglasses and stuff her hair into a black wool cap. They definitely couldn't warn her that Clotilda was headed this way, and that if Isabelle wanted to get to that secret meeting unnoticed, she'd be wise to use the back door instead.

But they couldn't. So she didn't.

She made it as far as the top of the stairs.

"For pity's sake, Isabelle," Clotilda said from the bottom of the stairs, "what are you wearing?"

Isabelle's sister preferred dressing like the fairy god-mothers from books, and tonight (despite the time) was no exception. She wore a long, silver gown that shimmered like the stars. Her slippers were adorned with sparkly pom-poms. And her hair was ridiculously perfect—not one stray hair out of place. It was tied neatly in a topknot bun—the very same way she wore it to greet her princesses. In her arms was a large tray, overflowing with cookies—and they smelled like cardamom, cinnamon, and Isabelle's favorite, chocolate.

They looked like they were still warm. "Are those for Roxanne? Are you getting ready to grant her a wish?"

"Actually," Clotilda said in her sweetest, most annoying voice, "I made them for you. I was hoping we could have a little sister time."

Sister time! That didn't sound like Clotilda, but there was a first time for everything.

Isabelle ran down the steps. She wondered what Clotilda wanted to talk about. She hoped it was the ring. But it was probably some mistake Isabelle had made. Clotilda often pointed out her errors.

She took a cookie and popped it into her mouth. *Mmmm.* The edges were crunchy. The chocolate melted in her mouth. She was about to take another when the grandmother clock chimed. It was ten minutes to midnight! She was late to meet Minerva.

"Can we meet a little bit later?" Isabelle asked in her

sweetest, most regretful voice. "I would love some sister time, but I have something important to attend."

Clotilda blocked her sister from moving. (This wasn't easy with a tray full of cookies.) "Like what?"

It was the middle of the night.

Isabelle was lurking in the castle hallway.

She was dressed like a bandit.

Even an average fairy godmother could see she was up to no good. And Clotilda wasn't average.

Isabelle didn't want to betray Minerva. So she asked, "Why are you up? Why the cookies? Is it because Grand-momma complained about me?" (These were valid questions, too, since Clotilda rarely stayed up late. She rarely made cookies. And when she did either of those things, it was for a princess. Not for her sister.)

Clotilda looked slightly offended. "I made them for you. Grandmomma said your wand work's looking great. She's very, very, very proud."

"Three *very*'s? Are you sure?" Isabelle took off her hat. She slid out of her shoes. Minerva would have to understand. (For cookies that smelled this good, she'd probably make the same choice herself.) Isabelle twirled three times as she followed her sister to her room. This was great news! Her grandmomma was proud! And that meant so was Clotilda!

"How is Roxanne?" she asked, checking out all Clotilda's trophies and ribbons and heartfelt testimonials. Knowing Clotilda, her new princess was already halfway to happily ever after.

"Nothing like Melody—that's for sure!" Melody, Clotilda's first official princess, was pretty much the definition of *easy peasy lemon squeezy*. She was kind. She liked horses. Her wishes had not made Clotilda sweat. "Roxanne wants so many things—and I don't mean matching pairs of riding boots." (Apparently, Melody had insisted on those.) "That girl wants to be in charge. As in actually run the government. She has so many ideas and plans, I can't decide which sparkles to use."

Roxanne sounded a lot like Nora. "I can't wait to learn about the colors."

"It's the best part of training," Clotilda said, reaching into her drawer for a rainbow-colored box. "The science of sparkles is logical. It's efficient. It gives you so much more wish control!" She tossed Isabelle a pair of hand-me-down goggles, slightly yellowed, then said, "Consider them yours."

After Isabelle put them on, Clotilda opened the box (probably just to show off). "They're vacuum sealed. To keep the sparkles fresh."

Isabelle liked the bright red sparkles best. "Are they for love?" Then she pointed to the royal-blue batch. "And are those for brains?"

"Isabelle, all princesses have brains." Clotilda opened her book to a huge expandable table called *The Official Guide to the Spectrum of Sparkles*. "As you can see, pure red is for girl power. Blue is for loyalty."

"What about green?" Isabelle asked, wondering if maybe now she could ask about the ring. "And what does yellow do?"

Clotilda pointed to a chart full of greens, from yellowish green to almost nearly blue. "The greens are all about integrity. Depending on the ratios of yellow and blue and sometimes white or even black, green can mean anything from responsibility to intuition." She pointed out the yellow section. "Yellow is simpler. It's the color of fear."

"Why do they need that?" Isabelle didn't think princesses feared anything.

Clotilda rolled her eyes. "Because fear is essential. It helps you stay out of trouble."

Isabelle was impressed with her sister's knowledge. She was also impressed with the teams of fairy godmothers who figured out what each color could do.

She was also scared. (There were a lot of colors to learn.)

Clotilda wasn't worried. "In Levels Three and Four, you'll learn the meaning of the colors. You'll learn some of the formulas. You'll find out that colors vary not just in purpose but also in power. For example, you only need a little royal blue to foster loyalty. But you can practically shower a princess in pink—and nobody will notice."

Isabelle pointed to a section wrapped in warning tape. "What's that for?"

"Pure orange sparkles," Clotilda said, "the most explosive, dangerous sparkle in the box." She explained, "Don't worry about it now. You won't touch anything orange until Level Four. If at all."

"What do you mean, if at all," Isabelle asked. "What does orange do?"

"It gives you confidence."

That didn't make sense to Isabelle. "I thought confidence was a good thing. Like gusto, right?"

"Confidence is a great thing," Clotilda said. "It's a lot like gusto . . . except it's stronger. And more powerful. And that means it's dangerous all by itself." When Isabelle looked more confused than ever, Clotilda started over.

"Think of it this way. Confidence paired with something like wisdom or empathy can help princesses to do great things. But on its own—watch out. Princesses with confidence and nothing else always think they're right. They don't listen to anyone. So they make lots of mistakes." She reached for her Wish List. "You want me to show you some examples?"

Isabelle didn't want to listen. Or read. She wanted to know exactly what some confidence felt like. "I want to try it! For tomorrow! It's a big day!"

Clotilda shook her head. She stifled a yawn. "You don't need confidence for tomorrow."

Isabelle was not going to take no for an answer. "If you give it to me, I'll leave you alone. I won't make any trouble."

Clotilda raised one eyebrow. She stifled another yawn. "Fine! I'll let you touch an orange sparkle, under these circumstances." She paused. "First, you have to promise to stay in your room until morning. And you can't tell Grandmomma." When Isabelle nodded, Clotilda added with a twinkle, "But most important, you have to promise to be very good and nice to me for the rest of our sisterhood. And next time, you're making the cookies."

"Yes!" She gave her sister a big hug. "I'll be nice to you forever! I'll make whatever you want!" She held out her hand, but Clotilda wasn't ready to shake on it.

"Seriously," she said, "if I let you touch an orange sparkle, will you promise to remember your glasses and your books? Will you thank Grandmomma for helping you learn everything you need to know for Level Three?"

When Isabelle promised to do all these things, Clotilda told her she'd let her try one. "But don't say I didn't warn you."

With her tweezers, Clotilda unwrapped the tape, picked up the tiniest orange sparkle, and touched Isabelle's arm. Right away, Isabelle's hands felt warmer. Her legs itched to run. She began to feel braver, and smarter, as though she knew what was best for the entire fairy godmother world— and no one could tell her otherwise.

Isabelle felt so confident, she forgot to say "thank you." Instead, she ran out the door and slid down the banister. Then she woke up Grandmomma to tell her that she was *soooooo* grateful and that she was going to be the best fairy godmother ever—even better than Clotilda. She made up a brand-new signature style—one that included three fancy moves: a swish of the wrist followed by a horizontal move to the sky and a high kick. She ran around the castle garden, shouting, "Keep calm and sparkle on," until Clotilda marched outside and dragged Isabelle back to her room.

In the morning, she felt like herself. (So mostly confident—but not totally.) Isabelle couldn't wait to get to class and learn! If she was worried about Minerva and the meeting she missed, it was only for a moment.

Minerva was not just a crabby old godmother. She was her friend. If Isabelle told her the truth, she'd understand.

At least, Isabelle hoped so.

Chapter Three

Worsts against Rules

*U*nfortunately, Minerva did not understand. Neither did Irene nor MaryEllen.

Isabelle felt every ounce of chocolate in the pit of her stomach. "What was I supposed to do? Clotilda stopped me on the stairs. She made a plate full of cookies. She wanted to have some sister time."

Minerva said, "We waited for two hours."

Irene said, "A good excuse is not an apology."

MaryEllen said, "You could have let us know."

There wasn't a fairy godmother alive who couldn't appreciate the importance of some sister time. But in this case, they knew Clotilda. "Your sister? And you? That's a good one!" MaryEllen and Irene cracked up into fits of croaky laughter.

Minerva, however, started pacing at an alarming speed. (She didn't believe in coincidences.) "What do you mean she stopped you on the stairs? What did you tell her? Did she ask you anything suspicious? About us?"

Isabelle promised she was just being nice—that the note never came up in conversation—not even once. "Besides, what could I have told her? I don't know what you're up to either."

"Shhhhhh!" Minerva said, leading Isabelle to some overgrown shrubbery and a new gnarly tree full of pink blossoms—not that different from the one she planted during Level Two. There she handed Isabelle a piece of purple paper folded to look like a lily. "This will explain everything," she said to Isabelle. "If you agree with any part of this, we're meeting again tonight."

Isabelle unfolded the paper flower and put on her glasses. At the top and down the sides, the purple parchment was decorated with sparkly flowers and vines. They felt soft—as if they were alive. But the word at the top of the page was anything but lovely.

*W.A.R.**

"War?" That didn't sound good.

"Not war. W.A.R.," Minerva said. "It's an acronym." She pointed to the bottom of the page.

Isabelle read, "*W.A.R.* stands for Worsts against Rules: an organization devoted to fairness among all fairy godmothers." She was pretty sure Grandmomma was going to have a conniption. "You couldn't think of something a little . . . nicer?"

Minerva told her to keep her voice down. "We're sick of being nice."

Irene added, "Why should we respect a bunch of mean fairy godmothers that call us the Worsts?"

Isabelle didn't want to argue (those mean fairy godmothers were her relatives), so instead, she continued reading. Lucky for Isabelle, the message was short. Even better, there was no fine print.

Are you unhappy with the way the Bests treat you? Dissatisfied with your stature and/or potential? Do you think the whole fairy godmother system stinks and needs a big reboot? If you do, we want to hear from you! We are determined to make things better for all fairy godmothers.

All fairy godmothers and trainees are welcome.

Minerva said, "It's good, right?" (That meant she wrote it herself.) "Are you in?"

Isabelle handed it back to her. "So it's a club? A chance to complain?"

Minerva pounded her cane into the ground. "For all that is sparkly, it's a movement! A revolution!" Dirt flew in all directions. "We're sick of being insulted. It's not fair that we always have to pick our princesses last. We are good fairy godmothers—honest fairy godmothers—and we've got experience, too. We're going to raise our voices so we can improve our lives and our princesses' lives, too. Or do you think everything is fine and dandy the way it is?"

Isabelle wasn't sure what to say. Of course, she had complaints about the fairy godmother world—her mom *had* been banished! But she also knew the Bests had good reasons for creating the rules (even Three C—the worst one of all). And even though Minerva had ignored her second practice princess and could have been banished, Grandmomma did not do it. Instead, she put her on secret probation. (Or, rather, just probation. It wasn't very secret, since everybody knew it.)

Isabelle wondered if Minerva had broken another rule. "Are you doing this because you're going to the Fairy Godmother Home for Normal Girls?"

"No! Of course not! This has nothing to do with the Home." Minerva paced with the speed of a much younger fairy godmother. "This is just a meeting. It's a chance to talk about issues we'd been thinking about even before we were sent to retraining. Will you come? It would mean a lot. All you have to do is listen."

Isabelle sighed. In the fairy godmother world, there was always listening. And waiting. And after that, more listening.

She was pretty sure she should say no, but she was also curious. "Why do you need me?" Isabelle asked. "I can't change anything."

"That's where you're wrong," Irene said.

MaryEllen added, "For this to work, we're going to need you to talk to your grandmomma."

"Talk to Grandmomma?" Isabelle asked. She looked at the sparkly door of the center. She wanted to go to training. She didn't want to talk about problems or tell her grandmomma what was going on.

"Forget about your grandmomma," Minerva said, giving her friends the stink eye. "Just come to the meeting. It'll be here. At midnight. After that, it's up to you. You don't have to do anything you don't want to."

Isabelle nodded. "Can I invite Fawn and Angelica? What about Clotilda?"

"No. Just you. Please don't tell anyone." Minerva thrust the flyer back into her hands. "Listen, I get it. You're young. You're smart enough. You're just learning the ropes. *War* is a very dramatic word. But when you're my age, you figure out that you have to use dramatic words if you want people to listen."

She promised two more times that it was just a meeting— nothing more. "Then we can talk."

As Isabelle started for the door, Minerva added, "Doing the right thing is never easy. You don't always get what you want. There is only one thing I can promise you: No one ever regrets it."

Chapter Four

A Very Good Beginning

Isabelle was relieved to get away from the Worsts. With as much gusto as she could muster, she pulled the READY door wide open and strutted into the center.

The first thing she saw was her favorite sign: HAPPILY EVER AFTER: THE LAST LINE OF EVERY GREAT STORY. It was in its rightful place—on the wall behind Grandmomma's desk—and unlike last time, the picture was level. The jar of candy was back on the desk, too. And it was full of Grandmomma's favorite treats.

Angelica and Fawn were already checking out all the new pictures and slogans. "Welcome back," Isabelle said. "How was your vacation?"

"Totally boring!" Angelica complained.

Fawn said, "Unhappily magic free!"

They raised their empty wands above their heads and touched stars. Then they twirled once and burst into giggles. Isabelle should have felt nothing but happiness. She was here. Angelica and Fawn were happy to see her. But something was bugging her, and it wasn't just the Worsts. Even though her friends were being perfectly nice, they'd changed—even more than she had—especially on the outside.

In other words, they looked older.

Their lips were painted bright pink—just like Clotilda's. Fawn's dress resembled a brilliant rainbow. Her hair looked sleek and smooth—more like Kaminari's every day. Angelica was different, too. She was now a full head taller than her friend. And stronger-looking—if that was possible. She'd also dyed the tips of her braids bright red, and bright gold—Luciana's favorite colors. It seemed to make her dark skin glow.

Isabelle looked down at her regular dress and regular sneakers with scuffs on the soles. She was wearing no makeup. Her hair was just as messy as always.

(In the fairy godmother world, just like the regular one, confidence is temporary. It is easy to get down on yourself for stupid reasons like clothes or even no reason at all.)

Angelica noticed that Isabelle looked sad. (She assumed it was because of all the fussing during Level Two—not her clothes.) "Don't worry," she said to Isabelle. "This time, we'll all help each other. If we make a mistake, we will figure it out together."

Fawn added, "That's what the science of sparkles is all about." To prove her point, she pointed to the new slogans on the wall.

ALWAYS QUESTION. ALWAYS WONDER.

And

SCIENCE CAUSES ALL KINDS OF REACTIONS.

And the best one:

THE SCIENCE OF SPARKLES. MEASURE TWICE. CUT ONCE.

It included a warning:

DO NOT ATTEMPT ANYTHING WITHOUT FIRST DONNING YOUR
PROTECTIVE GEAR.

Angelica whipped out a pair of goggles, monogrammed with the letter *A*. Fawn owned a pair, too. Except hers were monogrammed with an *F*. Isabelle showed them the goggles Clotilda had given her. Even though they weren't mono-grammed or new or clean, they were deemed the best because they once belonged to Clotilda. That made Isabelle feel a little bit better. But not totally better.

She wanted to impress her friends.

So Isabelle told them about the apple and Grand-momma's collection of shoes, and then (even though she promised not to tell anyone), she bragged about Clotilda giving her the orange sparkle. When they didn't quite believe that Clotilda would break that rule, she almost told them about W.A.R. But something stopped her. So instead, she took the ring out of her pocket. "I think it belonged to my mom." (She was positive this would do the trick.)

She was right! "This is amazing," Angelica said.

"Brilliant," Fawn said. "And probably illegal." They told her to put it away—but not before they each tried it on.

"What do you think it can do?" Angelica whispered, holding it up toward the light to maximize its sparkliness. "Do you really think your mom used this on her unhappy princess?"

Isabelle didn't want to talk about the unhappiness princess that got her mom banished from the fairy godmother world. She also didn't want to lie. "I wish I could tell you, but I don't know! I tried for hours, and I couldn't get it to do anything."

This was a bit disappointing. And slightly awkward. So Isabelle took the ring from Angelica and put it back in her pocket. The trainees turned their attention to things they could discuss with authority—the photos from the Extravaganza.

There was a great one of the three of them. The class shot would have been perfect, too, except that Minerva was scowling, and Irene was holding rabbit ears above Mary-Ellen's head.

Fawn frowned. "Those Worsts! When we walked in the door, they didn't even say hello."

"If you ask me," Angelica said, "the Bests should have banished them—for good."

Isabelle was glad she hadn't said anything about W.A.R. "Give them a chance. Level Two *was* terrible." Then both doors flew open.

The Worsts filed in.

Grandmomma followed right behind them.

When they saw Grandmomma, Isabelle, Angelica, and Fawn scrambled to their desks. They curtsied in the traditional way. "So sparkly to see you," they said in unison.

If you asked Isabelle, Grandmomma looked more serene than sparkly. Her lavender robe gave her a queenly demeanor. Her wand looked extra-long today, too, but maybe that was Isabelle's imagination at work.

"Good morning, trainees," Grandmomma said. "So sparkly to see you, too." She opened her candy jar and offered each trainee (including the Worsts) a peppermint patty (her favorite). "Welcome to Level Three. It's so nice to be back and even nicer to see all of you here. First, I'd like to apologize for missing your Level Two training, but as I'm sure you all know, it couldn't be helped. Second, I want to ensure you that we are going to have a wonderful time introducing you to the science of sparkles. I also want to say how proud I am. You are halfway through. That last level was particularly challenging. It's clear to me you are all going to be wonderful fairy godmothers."

Grandmomma might seem harsh. She definitely had high standards. But she would do anything for the fairy god-mother world. Isabelle was 99.9 percent sure she had never sounded so happy. She believed in happily ever after. And in them.

Isabelle wished she could tear up the Worsts' flyer. But she couldn't do anything now. (Grandmomma was talking.)

"Before I invite the Bests to return, I also want to thank you from the bottom of my heart. And for that matter, I'd like to offer kudos to your princesses. They all acted like superheroes. And you were all grace under pressure. Even you, Minerva." She clapped her hands until Angelica, Fawn, and Isabelle (but not the Worsts) were smiling. "I also want to reassure you that never again will any of you have to worry about mischief interfering with your wishes. While you were in training, I took inventory of every single sparkle and every single fairy godmother, past, present, and future, and we have officially contained the leak. What happened in Level Two will never happen again."

Everyone in the room stood up and cheered for Grandmomma. One by one, each trainee shook her hand.

Minerva stood behind Isabelle as Angelica shook Grandmomma's hand (and went on and on about how amazing she was). "This doesn't change anything," she whispered. "I know you agree with us. See you tonight."

When they were all seated, Grandmomma raised her wand. One flick produced a shower of flower petals. Candles lit up the room. "So today, let's put our books away. Instead, I'd like to begin Level Three with a celebration. I want the chance to talk to each of you, one on one." She pointed to the door, and everyone turned. "And so do the Bests."

Chapter Five

A Not-So-Good Middle

The Bests knew how to make an entrance.

Today, they wore sparkly oven mitts and aprons, sensible shoes, and shiny chef hats. That was because they carried large tureens of the most delicious foods Isabelle had ever seen or smelled.

She couldn't wait to taste it all!

Luciana entered first. *"Hola, estudiantes!"* she said. Right away, Isabelle smelled fresh tomato. And garlic. And a dash of hot pepper. Luciana said, "Wait until you try my first princess's paella. You'll swear it came straight from the ocean."

Raine's tray was piled high with one of Grandmomma's all-time favorite dishes, piri piri chicken. Kaminari followed with dumplings and pork buns and fresh vegetables with spicy dipping sauce. And Clotilda carried barbecued brisket with hush puppies and extra sauce for dipping. Then they all ran back for another tray of Grandmomma's favorites treats, from chocolate twigs to peppermint patties to cheeses, breads, and cookies, and steaming cups of hot chocolate and cider.

Now, this was the perfect way to start training. As she ate, Isabelle convinced herself that Minerva was happy, too—that she would throw away that flyer and cancel the meeting.

But before she could find out, the worst thing happened. In her enthusiasm to get in line for another bowl full of chicken, Isabelle bumped her desk. Every single paper and book tumbled to the ground.

This was a very serious problem. Not because accidents never happened in the fairy godmother world. But because important books were never supposed to fall on the floor. (According to the rule book, dropping books was an act of ultimate disrespect.)

Even worse, Isabelle accidentally kicked her Wish List— her most sacred book of all—and it slid across the floor to Grandmomma's feet. Of course, because bad things always happened in threes, the book popped open to the page where she'd hidden the folded-up flyer about W.A.R.

Grandmomma stooped to pick up the pretty purple lily. At first, she looked amused—as if this were a game—as if she was expecting to find a silly drawing or something else that would be equally embarrassing. She might even have thought the paper was a thank-you card that Isabelle had been passing around.

(If only it had been that!)

Isabelle quickly shouted, "Don't read it, Grandmomma. Please!"

Unfortunately, in the fairy godmother world (just as in the regular one), when someone says, "Don't read," they might as well say, "Read as soon as possible." Even the word *please* can't change that.

So Grandmomma unfolded the paper and smoothed it out on her desk. As she read, her eyes opened wide, and her lip quivered—but only for a second.

Grandmomma was a godmother with very strong magic. She was a godmother with standards. But just in case it wasn't clear, she was a mother first and foremost. She loved the center and the fairy godmother world. She had devoted her whole life to making it better.

So she did not reach for her wand.

She did not raise her voice.

But Minerva did. She stepped up onto her chair, whipped out her wand, and shouted, "Elizabeth Marie, with all due respect, what you have in your hands is just the beginning. And it's not just me, Irene, and MaryEllen that are concerned. There are many others who would like to see you change the way we do things around here. We believe that the system isn't fair and will be stronger with improvements. Will you sit down and talk with us? We have a lot of ideas. I don't think you'll disagree with any of them."

Grandmomma stared at the paper. Minerva stared at Grandmomma. Isabelle didn't know who to stare at, but she hoped Grandmomma would say yes.

Unfortunately, she didn't.

Instead, she crumpled the flyer into a ball and threw it on the floor. Then she whipped out her wand. "Perhaps we should stop celebrating and begin today's lesson."

Minerva stepped down from her chair. She picked up her things. She said, "No, thank you. I'd rather not." Then she walked out the door with an audible huff. Irene and MaryEllen (quietly) followed her.

The rest of them sat still. They said nothing. The Worsts had never acted against the Bests before. Isabelle was pretty sure the food was turning cold.

Grandmomma told the Bests to pack things up and meet her in her office. She told the trainees to go home. Then she held her wand high. "Class dismissed!"

Chapter Six

The Manifesto

All afternoon and night, Isabelle could hear footsteps, slamming doors, and all sorts of voices in the castle. Some of the voices sounded angry. Some of the voices were scared. Some of them sounded familiar. But not all of them. Some of them were voices and accents and languages she'd never heard before.

The only voices she was sure of were Grandmomma's deep, authoritative voice—and Luciana's passionate ups and downs. At one point, she heard a crash, followed by a lot of yelping and screaming. Then she thought she heard Minerva. That gave her hope. Maybe they were in the middle of creating a treaty.

Since she couldn't stand the suspense, she sneaked all the way to Grandmomma's office door and put her ear on the tiny peephole right underneath the lion's mouth, but she couldn't hear more than sounds and whispers and groans.

This was the problem with thick walls! (And knowing Grandmomma, probably some kind of magic.)

Isabelle was about to head to the kitchen for a snack when she noticed a shadow. She was not alone. Clotilda was standing quietly at the next door. Her ear was pressed against a water glass, and the glass was pressed against the wall.

Isabelle whispered, "Does that actually work?"

Clotilda startled easily when she was sneaking around. "No," she said, putting down the glass and gaining some composure. "Not really." Then she dragged her sister down the dark hall to Isabelle's bedroom so they could talk without whispering.

Clotilda went first. "Why do you think the Worsts are so upset? Do you know what they want? You weren't in on this, were you?"

Isabelle promised she wasn't. She was also pretty sure Minerva didn't want to go on strike. "They told me they were meeting tonight at the center. Maybe we should go talk to them."

Clotilda liked the idea of saving the fairy godmother world from unnecessary misery and delay. If that happened, she might be named third-best! Or even higher! She said, "Why don't we pack up some cookies and go see what they're up to?" She believed that everyone was more cooperative when something warm and chocolaty was involved.

It was a good idea.

They got some cookies and a rule book and walked to the center. Along the way, they practiced what they would say. Things like:

a) We value your contributions.

b) We won't call you the Worsts.

c) We will get Grandmomma to listen.

But when they got there, it was d) too late. The Worsts were not in the mood for listening to Isabelle and Clotilda. (They had already made a lot of decisions.)

Irene said, "Maybe if you'd come earlier."

MaryEllen said, "But you didn't, so we decided to get your grandmomma's attention a different way."

Clotilda refused to take no for an answer. She opened her rule book to the section on bylaws (another name for rules) and pointed to a page titled *When You Have Complaints*.

She showed them the fine print as well as the forms to fill out. "If you express your concerns the official way, they are more likely to be noticed by the Bests."

Minerva laughed. She took a cookie and tossed aside the book. "Thanks but no, thanks," she said with a full mouth. "Forms get lost. They get stuck at the bottom of the pile. We want change now. We're tired of waiting."

All the way home, Clotilda moped. (She was not used to failure, but she refused to give up hope.) "Tomorrow, Grandmomma will listen to them. They'll make their demands and Grandmomma will do her best. They'll have to see that she cares about nothing more than the fairy godmother world."

"And if not?" Isabelle asked.

"And if not, she has a lot of sparkle power. And as we all know, she's not afraid to use it."

The next morning, Isabelle and Clotilda arrived at the training center early, but not early enough. Angelica and Fawn hovered under the gnarly tree. Minerva, Irene, and MaryEllen stood in front of the doors. Facing them were Grandmomma, Luciana, Kaminari, and Raine.

Grandmomma and the Bests were tall and grandly dressed. They all carried wands that were full of sparkles.

The Worsts were old. They had no sparkles. But they didn't seem to care.

"Will you come back to training?" Grandmomma asked.

Minerva shook her head. "Not until you listen to our demands."

"Are you still calling yourselves W.A.R.?" Luciana asked.

Minerva nodded. "But we're not waging war." As the Bests grumbled, Irene and MaryEllen distributed pamphlets to everyone there—including all the trainees. "Last night, we sat down and wrote this manifesto" (in other words, a piece of paper filled with demands). The manifesto said:

We, the undersigned believe the following:

Although the Official Rule Book for Fairy Godmothers *was not written with bad intentions, it is our belief that the rules have created an unfair society of haves and have-nots. We suspect that all fairy godmothers (ie: not just the Worsts) would benefit from reviewing the rules and revising them to make them fairer to all godmothers—not just the ones at the top of the Best list.*

In response, we have created this manifesto. Its purpose is to restore equality and fairness to all fairy godmothers.

Here are our official demands:

1. *In the fairy godmother world, the terms Best and Worst will from this moment forward be eliminated and never used again, even in jest.*

2. *Princess selection will become random, based on a lottery system that gives each and every fairy godmother an equal chance for any one princess.*

3. *Retraining, when necessary, will be created on an individual basis—to help the godmother, not embarrass her.*

4. *Our castles need attention! The drafts at the last Extravaganza made the whole party unpleasant.*

Sincerely,
The very competent godmothers you call the Worsts

"I told you they should have made them retire," Angelica muttered.

"They're going to ruin everything," Fawn said.

Isabelle held her ring in her pocket. She wished on the ring and all that was sparkly that Grandmomma would listen to Minerva. Or offer a compromise. Or that she could go back in time and show up at that meeting. If she had, she might have been able to talk them out of this.

Unfortunately, fairy godmother magic didn't work that way. The ring didn't do anything. The damage was done.

Minerva asked, "Will you think about our demands?"

Instead of yes or no. Grandmomma asked Clotilda to take the young trainees to their castle for a light lunch. "While we work this out, I think it would be nice to give Angelica and Fawn the official tour. Then settle them in for some fun and games. In fact, settle them in for the night!" She smiled as though this was no big deal. "I'm sure this will all be settled *lickety-split*."

But she meant, "Please get them out of here. Now. And don't come back until morning."

Chapter Seven

The Sleepover Party, Part One

When they arrived at the castle, Clotilda gathered the three trainees on the front steps. "Before we go inside, I have a few things to tell you."

When Clotilda said *a few things*, she usually meant *a few rules*. Or probably *a lot of rules* that added up to no fun.

Isabelle didn't want to hear it—not when they had the whole castle to themselves! "Can you tell us later?" she asked. "I want to take them to Grandmomma's office to see the Official Fairy Godmother Spyglass and the spinning wheel and also the magic mirror."

To the disappointment of all three trainees, Clotilda said that would be impossible. "This castle is filled with very advanced and complicated magic. It is also one of the oldest fairy godmother residences in this part of the fairy godmother world and must be treated with respect." She looked a bit smug. "So don't touch anything that looks fragile. And stay away from the locked rooms—especially the office."

"Are you kidding me?" Isabelle asked. "But that's the best—"

"Sorry," Clotilda said, not looking or sounding sorry at all, "but under the circumstances, Grandmomma's office is definitely off-limits." She blocked the entrance. "Can you all agree to these terms?"

Even though this sounded like the most boring sleepover ever, the trainees agreed. Clotilda opened the door and led them into the giant foyer. The smell of lemon was in the air. "Let's go to the kitchen," Isabelle said, also getting a whiff of ginger and possibly a dash of vanilla. She didn't think she had to explain that good smells meant good treats.

But apparently, she did, because Fawn was more interested in staring at an old painting of a fairy godmother granting a wish. And Angelica seemed delighted to talk to Clotilda about an ancient rusted cauldron. Isabelle couldn't believe she had to drag them down the hall. Who didn't understand that lemon-ginger bars were better warm than cold?

After two bars and a handful of chocolate sticks each, Angelica noticed a big black door just outside the kitchen. It was held fast by a star-shaped gold lock. "Where does *that* go?" she asked Clotilda. "Don't tell me. Somewhere we can't go?"

"That's the door to the basement," Isabelle said.

"What's in it?"

"I don't know."

Angelica couldn't believe it. "You don't know what's in your own basement?"

"Ask Clotilda," Isabelle said. "She's been there a zillion times."

Clotilda pulled a large golden key from her pocket. "That's because I'm a Best. And unfortunately, you're not."

Fawn jiggled the lock and ate another cookie. She said, "It's no big deal" (even though it obviously was). "Kaminari told me your basement is really boring. And that it's a total mess—because your grandmomma is a slob!"

Mentioning Kaminari made Clotilda turn bright pink, since the Bests were very competitive with each other. "That's just gossip," she said. "It's not true at all."

Fawn furrowed her brow. "Kaminari also said your grandmomma has something living down there. But she won't tell anyone what it is."

That made Clotilda laugh. "Of course there's something living down there."

The trainees stepped back. "There is?"

"Yes," Clotilda said. "Frogs."

Isabelle almost fell over. "In my own castle? How many?"

When Clotilda said she couldn't be sure since the population changed all the time, the trainees begged to see them. They'd all grown up hearing countless stories about frogs and princesses. Plus, frogs were cute. Not as cute as kittens, of course. But better than spiders or rats or other types of animals that always seemed to be associated with basements and magic.

Isabelle pulled her sister out of earshot. "It's my first sleepover! I want them to like me. Why can't you understand?"

Clotilda did understand. (It hadn't been that long since her days as a trainee.)

"Okay," she said. "You don't need to twist my arm. Put on some protective gear. I'll take you to the basement."

Very quickly (before Clotilda could change her mind), they donned shiny, white coveralls, goggles, masks to cover their noses and mouths, gloves, and what looked like some of Grandmomma's old shower caps.

There were also more rules:

- Don't touch anything—especially closed boxes and lids.

- Stay away from anything with warning tape. Especially if it says *LIVE*.

- Be careful where you're stepping.

- Only go as far as the frogs. No farther!

Clotilda tried to make her voice sound scary. "Also: Watch out for the mice."

"Mice!" Isabelle loved mice. "Can we pet them?"

"Were you not listening to anything I said?" Clotilda asked. "I repeat, do not touch anything. Not mice. Not frogs. Not anything else." Clotilda opened up the creaking door. In front of them was a steep, winding, spiral staircase that looked in dire need of repair. "Okay. Except the rail. That, you should touch."

One by one, they slowly followed Clotilda one step at a time. After about a hundred steps, Isabelle's glasses turned frosty. At two hundred, it didn't matter, because everything was pitch-black. Now the steps felt softer and uneven, as if they were made of clay. They were also smaller. And it was hard to walk in the dark. Isabelle began to feel dizzy. She heard tiny footsteps. (Probably the mice.)

Fawn did not like mice. "Are those the—?"

"Yes. But don't worry. They don't like you, either. They climb the walls and play in the rafters," Clotilda said, snapping her wand. Candle sconces on every wall flicked on. The basement was like Grandmomma's office—except even messier. Isabelle gasped. "All this time, I thought you were joking about the basement. I had no idea all this stuff was down here."

Everywhere they looked, they saw boxes and shelves and stacks of books and dresses and many interesting trinkets. (The part about Grandmomma being a slob was definitely true.) Around the room, sparkles flickered off of the lights. There were also old, discarded girlgoyles propped up

against the wall. Some of them had chipped noses. Or missing limbs. Or heads.

Angelica pointed to an open box in the corner, right next
to a headless girlgoyle. "Can we touch those?"

The box was marked USED WANDS. COMPLETELY
HARMLESS.

Clotilda sighed. "Fine. If you want to play with some
old sticks, go ahead. They haven't had magic in them for
years."

Angelica and Fawn sifted through the pile. Most of them
were not much more than nubs and only one still had a
smidgen of a star at its tip.

Next to the wands was a large bookshelf stuffed to the
brim with chipped teacups, beakers of all sizes and shapes,
bowls, spoons, a couple of random shoes, and one tiara,
missing a few jewels.

Before Clotilda could stop her, Angelica picked it up and
plopped it onto her head. "Call me Princess Angelica," she

said to Isabelle and Fawn. "Where are those frogs? Bring me some mice. Who wants to grant my wish?"

Before Clotilda could snatch the tiara off her head, Fawn picked up a pink feather duster and pretended to tidy up. Isabelle, who had never really understood the connection between princesses and chores, found something more interesting (and probably dangerous). It was a small box wrapped in warning tape, and just in case that wasn't clear enough, it was also labeled DO NOT TOUCH. Isabelle wanted to check it out, but before she could make her move, Clotilda flicked her wand. *Poof, poof, poof!* The tiara, duster, and box disappeared. She said, "If you want to see some frogs, let's see some frogs."

The trainees knew they were in trouble, so without complaining, they followed her down a decline to the southeast corner of the basement and some standing pond scum. Clotilda said, "When visiting frogs, it's best not to make sudden noises."

"Why's that?" Fawn asked.

"Because some of them are shy." Clotilda waved her wand in a swirling motion to create a bit of sunlight. "Hello, there," she said in a soft and gentle voice. "Anybody up for a chat?"

A second later, Fawn pointed to some bubbles. They all heard a few croaks. Then they saw a splash.

Two frogs, one reddish, one greenish, jumped out of the water near Clotilda's feet. The reddish one managed a back-flip, as if he wanted some attention. The greenish one looked sort of lazy and a bit on the chubby side. But otherwise, they looked like any old frogs you'd find at a lake or pond or swamp.

Clotilda pointed to the green one. "Trainees, this is Cornelius. And the red one is Harry." She said to the frogs, "Now that they've seen you, you can go about your business. These girls aren't official yet. They have no use for frogs."

Cornelius jumped back into the pond, but Harry didn't move.

"Am I seeing things, or is that frog pouting?" Angelica asked.

Clotilda confirmed that, indeed, Harry was pouting. That was because the greenish ones were regular frogs. But the red ones (like Harry) were frogs that were waiting to be kissed.

Isabelle couldn't believe it. "You mean frogs really can turn into princes? It's not just an old story?"

"Officially, it's not that simple," Clotilda said (as if anything was). "As you know, princesses used to believe that evil witches turned princes into frogs. That was nonsense, of course, but a very good story. So we came up with a deal. In return for this lovely pond and others all over the fairy godmother world, the frogs help us out when we need them. One kiss per frog. One princess per kiss."

This was unbelievably cool. "Can we feed them?" Fawn asked. "Or pet them?"

"I don't recommend it," Clotilda said. "Some of those red ones have been waiting a long time. If you so much as hold out your hand, you never know what might happen."

Since nobody wanted to risk it, they all took a step back. And then another. And another. Then Clotilda led them to the stairs. (She was tired of playing tour guide.) "As I recall, our deal was just for the frogs." She herded them back through the basement and back up the stairs.

As they disposed of their protective gear in the kitchen, Clotilda told them they were on their own. "Go get yourselves some snacks and show your friends the girlgoyles. Or better yet, play some party games." She reminded them of the rules (no touching anything—especially anything that might break; no going to the office or past any other closed doors; and no sneaking around). She reminded them that Grandmomma could return home any time. "She won't tolerate any shenanigans—especially when there are so many other shenanigans going on already."

Fawn said, "You don't have to tell us."

Angelica crossed her heart. "We wouldn't dream of causing any trouble."

As soon as Clotilda was gone, they grabbed some snacks and dashed up the stairs to Isabelle's room.

(It was hard not to giggle.)

Shenanigans were exactly what they had in mind.

Chapter Eight

The Sleepover Party, Part Two

While they waited for Grandmomma to return (and go to sleep—hopefully, as soon as possible), Isabelle, Angelica, and Fawn braided one another's hair. They also played cards and told each other scary stories of godmothers who made terrible mistakes (but, thankfully, weren't Mom). Then they pretended their wands were microphones, and sang and danced to their favorite songs. When Cornelius (the green frog) wriggled out from under the covers, Fawn jumped up and yelled, "Get him out of here!"

Frogs in a frog pond were cute. But in a bedroom—not so much. Plus, Cornelius looked scared. And a bit out of sorts. They had to catch him—before Clotilda did.

To their surprise, once they started chasing him, Cornelius was fast. And slippery, too. They followed him out the door and through the hall and downstairs into the kitchen. Luckily, he had no use for dishes or human snacks or fragile fairy godmother collectibles! All he wanted was to go outside to the pond. When the trainees realized this, they opened the door, and off he went.

Back in Isabelle's room, they burst into giggles. "What were you thinking?" Fawn whispered.

Angelica said, "I wanted to hide him in Clotilda's room. Can you imagine? It would have been so funny."

Fawn had also been up to mischief. "I stole something, too." She dug deep into her pocket and pulled out a smidgen of teeny tiny sparkles.

"Where'd you find those?" Isabelle asked.

"I shook them out of the duster," Fawn said. "Sparkles

get stuck there all the time. Even when your grandmomma isn't a slob."

Angelica patted her friend on the back. "Good thinking," she said. "What should we do first?"

"Nothing right now," Fawn said, to Isabelle and Angelica's dismay. "We have to wait for the magic hour, of course. Or for Isabelle's grandmomma to come home and go to bed."

Fawn was the number one trainee. She didn't want to get caught by Grandmomma.

Luckily, they didn't have to wait that long. Grandmomma returned well before the magic hour. Unluckily, she did not go straight to her room. First, she stomped around the castle. Then she had a snack. Then she took a long bath (they could hear her singing). And then finally, she went to bed.

When the trainees were 99 percent sure Grandmomma was sleeping (they could hear her snoring), they turned on the light. And pulled out the sparkles.

There were nine of them. All multicolor.

Angelica rubbed her hands together. "What should we do first?"

Isabelle had a great idea. "We could climb up to the tower and look at the stars and toss wishes into the sky."

"No offense," Fawn said, "but I want to play Truth or Dare."

"That would be stupendous," Angelica said. She turned to Isabelle. "Do you mind if I go first?"

"Not at all," Isabelle said. Truth or Dare was one of those games that sounded more fun than it was. She reminded her friends that in terms of sparkles, Grandmomma had a way of finding out everything—even when Isabelle thought she had been really sneaky.

Angelica and Fawn weren't worried about being caught. Fawn told Isabelle, "If you're worried, take a truth. Or we could dare you to do something that didn't require sparkles."

Angelica said, "But what would be the fun of that?" Then she took two sparkles from Fawn. "Dare me to do something really good." She told Isabelle, "You'll see. No one will care if we make a little sparkly mischief."

Fawn paced in a circle. "I dare you," she said, "to sneak into Clotilda's room and turn her hair green."

Isabelle had to admit that was a great dare! She pictured Clotilda waking up and seeing her new shiny, green hair in the mirror. She was going to be so mad!

Together, they crept down the hall to Clotilda's room. Then they listened at her bedroom door—just in case she was still awake. When they heard nothing, they opened her door. It was dark inside. And completely still. Angelica pointed to a lumpy form under the blankets. "*Shhhhh*, she's sleeping." She loaded a sparkle into her wand and bravely raised it over Clotilda's sleeping face. "This is going to be easy peasy lemon—huh?"

Something was wrong. Or, rather—someone was missing.

Angelica flicked on the lights. Clotilda wasn't in bed. She'd stuffed her bed with pillows. "How did she know we were coming?"

Isabelle had no idea, but she did know that her sister's wand and sparkles were missing. So were her best shoes. "I bet she's out taking care of Roxanne."

She was sort of relieved. Clotilda loved her hair. Also: Now they could play something else.

But Angelica didn't want to stop. "Fawn, what do you want? Truth or dare?"

"The dare, of course!" Fawn said.

Angelica rubbed her hands together. "I dare you to sneak into the office and spy on Clotilda. Let's use that spyglass Isabelle was bragging about."

Isabelle felt a bit insulted. "I didn't brag . . . that much." When they insisted she bragged all the time about a lot of things (but especially the spyglass), she gave in and led them downstairs to the big red door with the brass handle and the lion knocker.

Tonight, the lion's teeth looked sharper than usual. But Fawn didn't seem bothered. She waved her wand in front of the lock until it clicked. Then she pushed the door open a crack. And then a tiny bit more. Since the room appeared to be empty, she walked inside, turned on the light, and yelped, "For all that is sparkly!"

(The room wasn't empty.)

Clotilda stood at the spyglass. "What are you three doing here?" She told them to be quiet. "For pity's sake, you don't want to wake up Grandmomma, do you?"

Fawn immediately began apologizing—in a very over-the-top fashion. "We are so sorry to disturb you. We were just playing Truth or Dare. We didn't mess up Roxanne's wish, did we?"

Clotilda said, "No, you didn't," in her sweetest voice, but Isabelle knew that this was a bluff. The spyglass wasn't for granting wishes—it was for watching. And spying. She was also pretty sure that Clotilda shouldn't be using it by herself—especially in the middle of the night. Also: If she were allowed to be here, she would not be acting so nice.

She would be mad.

Isabelle said, "Well, now that we're here, do you mind if we look around?" Then she whispered—just in case Clotilda wanted to trick her, "Or do I have to tell Grandmomma what you were up to?"

Clotilda didn't like being outsmarted by her little sister. "Take a look," she said, hands crossed over her chest. "But make it snappy." She smiled. "It's late."

As quickly as they could, the trainees examined the spinning wheel and the apple. Then they tried on every pair of shoes and washed their hands in the girlgoyle sink. Angelica sat in Grandmomma's chair. She said, "Welcome to training," and, "Minerva, you must be banished," in a deep Grandmomma-like voice. When they had each examined themselves in the mirror, Clotilda raised her wand. "Time's up. All of you need to go to bed!"

Angelica and Fawn did not agree. They dragged Isabelle back to the kitchen and, as quietly as possible (they didn't want to wake up Grandmomma either), devoured a bowl full of popcorn with caramel and honey-roasted nuts.

Isabelle hoped they could call it a night now. (For once, she agreed with Clotilda.) But Angelica and Fawn had other ideas. "We have six sparkles left," Angelica said. "And you haven't taken your turn."

Isabelle didn't want a dare. But she wanted a truth even less. "Okay," she said. "What do you want me to do?"

Angelica rubbed her hands together. She took a deep breath. And then she and Fawn turned very serious—like they'd been planning this a while. "We want to meet Nora. We dare you to take us to visit her." (They'd never seen a regular girl up close.)

This was a terrible idea. But Angelica and Fawn were determined—even if it meant getting into trouble.

"We'll take the blame," Angelica said.

Fawn added, "We'll help you in training."

Isabelle refused to do it. "I'll take the truth. I don't want to get in trouble. There is nothing you can say to make me break that rule."

But then Fawn asked the one question Isabelle could not deny. "Don't you want to see her, too?"

She was right. Isabelle did want to see Nora—more than anything. She missed her friend. Also, she couldn't shake that feeling that something was wrong.

So even though Isabelle was sure this was going to get her a one-way ticket to the Home for Normal Girls, she filled her wand with sparkles, raised her wand to the stars, and listened for Nora.

It didn't take long to hear her. She was singing the duet she had performed with Samantha during the play. Except it didn't sound like happy singing.

Now Isabelle was worried. She huddled with her friends. They raised their wands together.

Moments later, they found themselves on a gravel path in the middle of some dark woods.

This was a good sign. Happily ever after often happened in the middle of a deep, dark wood. There was only one problem: Nora wasn't here.

Chapter Nine

First-Day Jitters

As they walked through the woods, they heard laughter and shouting and talking and running around. They smelled chocolate and smoke. Up ahead was a huge wooden sign between two giant trees.

It said: WELCOME BACK, CAMPERS! FUN TIMES AHEAD! For lost campers (and now trainees), there was an arrow pointing them in the right direction. The three trainees took off down the path. At the end, they found a clearing with five small cabins, all made of wood and decorated with little flower beds near the entrances. They saw tons of regular girls—walking in and out of cabins, playing games, and singing songs. It looked like a lot of fun—perfect for Nora—like a mini Extravaganza. There were girls of all ages, sizes, shapes, and colors, and they all looked like they were having a great time.

The trainees hid behind the biggest, widest oak tree so they could find Nora without being found themselves. Also, they were nosy. There were a lot of regular girls to look at.

There was a girl with brown skin playing a guitar and leading songs near the campfire. A girl with bright purple hair spiked a ball over the volleyball net. There were girls rocking in hammocks and girls roasting marshmallows and a few of them were talking to three boys about something called the Tournament of Champions.

"Are you sure Nora is here?" Fawn asked. She didn't say what Isabelle was thinking: Was her magic off?

Isabelle closed her eyes and listened again. No. She could

hear Nora—and she was close. She started walking around the clearing, past the games and the singing and the campfire, and checked out each cabin. "She's here, and something's wrong."

Angelica looked back at the game. "I don't get it. How could something be wrong here? This place is great!"

Isabelle didn't think she had to explain that, like a lot of girls—even ones who act confident—Nora was serious and shy. Isabelle couldn't remember Nora ever talking about camp—or even wanting to go. In the summer, she liked hiking. And climbing trees. And singing.

At the fourth cabin, they found her sitting on a stoop by herself, picking petals off a daisy and reading a card. Isabelle felt a sharp pang in her heart. Nora's eyes looked pink around the edges. Her nose was red. She seemed to be holding her breath. In other words, she looked like she was using every single ounce of effort to hold back a big flood of tears.

Isabelle wanted to hug her friend. She wanted to assure her that camp seemed like fun. Or joke about the play. But she couldn't do that. Thanks to Rule Three C, Nora didn't recognize her.

All she could do was start from the beginning. "Hi," she said. "By any chance, is your name Nora?"

Angelica added, "We know your friend, Samantha. She told us to say hello." (Angelica was so smart.)

Now Nora smiled—a little bit. "She did? How do you know her?" Then she looked down at the card she was reading. "I wish she were here, too."

The word *wish* made all three trainees flinch. Isabelle said, "She told us about your play. And how great you are at singing. And Janet and Mason."

Nora pointed toward the path. "If you're looking for Mason, join the club. His bunk's down that path." Isabelle almost laughed. Nora thought the trainees were looking for boys!

It was hard to be nosy without making Nora suspicious—but Isabelle had to figure out what was wrong. "It must be fun to be here together."

Nora shrugged—not a good sign. "This is his third year at camp, so he has lots of friends besides me. And he also likes the tournament." She explained that the entire camp divided into four teams by colors: red, green, gold, and blue. For a whole week, they competed in everything—from sports to team songs. "On the last day, there's a race. And an awards ceremony. Mason says it's really fun."

This didn't seem that bad. "Will you be on the same team?"

Nora didn't think so. "The captains pick the teams. Since Mason is really good at sports, he'll be picked first. When they find out I stink, I'll probably be picked last."

Isabelle started to reach for her wand, but that was a bad idea, so she fiddled with the ring—just to keep her hands busy.

When Nora saw the ring, her eyes widened. She reached under her collar and pulled out a similar ring she wore on a leather rope. "It's my stepmom's," she said. "She gave it to me for my birthday. And so I wouldn't miss her that much."

"Your birthday?" the trainees said at once. They all knew that birthday wishes were powerful wishes. "When was it?"

"It's coming up. On the last day of the tournament."

Now Isabelle understood. Nora didn't just miss her family, Samantha, and Janet. She was going to miss them on her birthday.

Angelica and Fawn patted Nora on the back. They put the rings side by side.

They were a lot alike, but instead of Isabelle's yellow and green stones and the engravings on the sides, Nora's had all red stones and a little flower engraved on the side.

That gave Isabelle an idea. It gave Fawn and Angelica an idea, too. And it was the same idea for each. "Want to try on mine?" Isabelle asked. "It's a lucky ring, too. It might even make the tournament seem fun."

Nora laughed at Isabelle. (Her stepmom had said the same thing.)

"Yes! Try it on!" Angelica and Fawn said together. "Or better yet, trade! Maybe your ring will be lucky for Isabelle, too."

Isabelle put Nora's on first. It was very sparkly. "Fancy," she said.

"Not really," Nora said. "My stepmom got it in the mail. She said it was a copy of a famous princess's ring. Totally fake."

Then Nora tried on Isabelle's. "Look," Nora said, holding out her hand. "It's a mood ring." To the trainees' surprise, the stones now glistened deep, pure, perfect orange—the color of confidence—the one color Clotilda had warned Isabelle never to use alone.

Nora took off the ring and handed it back to Isabelle. "Now you put it on. Let's see if it changes back."

Right away, it did. The ring turned back to yellow and green.

Isabelle felt her stomach turn upside down. There must be sparkles in the ring! Even worse, Nora looked different—radiant and energized, and to Isabelle's dismay, full of confidence. She got up and said, "You know what? I think I'll go inside and introduce myself. See you around! You want to come in?"

The trainees declined as politely and quickly as possible. Coming here had been a dare. And the longer they stayed, the better the chance they were going to be caught. They might already be in trouble—thanks to the ring.

When they arrived back in Isabelle's room, they sat down on her bed. Isabelle placed the ring on a pillow. "Try it on," she said to them. "See if it changes."

"I don't think so," Angelica said.

Fawn refused to touch it. "It's not for me."

Instead, Angelica paged through her book for anything about magic rings. But she couldn't find a thing. Not even in the fine print.

Fawn, however, did find dire warnings about something else. "Unapproved magic between levels is definitely a first-class offense. And anything having to do with orange is highly discouraged."

Angelica hoped this wouldn't count. "We aren't technically between levels. She only wore the ring for a moment. And we don't know for sure that the ring can do anything. Plus," she said, turning to Isabelle, "you didn't know what you were doing—so maybe Grandmomma won't be mad."

This was not reassuring advice.

But there was nothing more they could do. So they said good night.

As Angelica and Fawn fell asleep, Isabelle stared at the ceiling. She was worried about Nora. She was also worried about the Worsts. (She hadn't forgotten them.)

When she couldn't sleep at all, she got up and made a wish of things she wanted to be true:

a) The ring was just a mood ring.

b) The Worsts would stop complaining.

c) They could begin learning the science of sparkles soon. Like, maybe tomorrow.

Most of all, she hoped that d) Nora was happy—that she had introduced herself and had a fun night and now had lots of friends, and that she and Mason were picked for the same team. Isabelle hoped Nora's birthday would be a great one and that any sort of confidence from the ring was only good.

That couldn't be too much to ask, could it?

Chapter Ten

This Is What Democracy Looks Like

The next morning, the trainees pretended that nothing strange had happened. They got ready, ate breakfast, and headed to the training center without mentioning the science of sparkles, Truth or Dare, or especially the ring. That might jinx their luck.

They really wanted to start training.

What they found was not encouraging: fairy godmothers from every corner of the fairy godmother world either shouting, pumping fists, carrying signs—or all three! Although many of the older godmothers sat, most of them marched back and forth in front of the center's doors.

"What a catastrophe," Fawn said.

Angelica threw her books on the ground. (That's how mad she was.) "Those Worsts have really done it now."

One by one, the three climbed up onto a branch of the gnarly tree. There was a lot to see. They didn't want to miss anything.

Some of the signs were very beautiful. They looked like they were made of sparkles. But none of the trainees had ever heard slogans like these.

Zahara's sign said: THERE IS NO SUCH THING AS A WORST FAIRY GODMOTHER.

Irene's said: FIGHT LIKE A GODMOTHER.

MaryEllen's said: I AM HAVING A VERY BAD DAY.

Minerva's was the biggest. It said: SPARKLY BUT BITTER.

There were others that said things like UNFAIR and RESIST and EQUAL RIGHTS FOR ALL GODMOTHERS, and one godmother held a sign that said RESPECT THE POWER OF SPARKLES, which wasn't technically in dispute in the fairy godmother world, but it looked good on the sign.

When Raine and Kaminari arrived, Minerva stood on a sparkly soapbox and shouted into her megaphone. "Sparkly but bitter. Sparkly but bitter!" And everyone else shouted back, "Experience is everything! We will not be overlooked!"

Particularly upsetting were the numbers of godmothers who weren't Worsts. Fawn pointed to a lanky, dark-haired godmother in a brightly colored dress. "Isn't that Galina?" She had become one of the most highly respected fairy god-mothers after making a famous ballerina H.E.A. They also noticed an older brown-skinned fairy godmother wearing a traditional sari covered in jewels. Her name was Riya, and if there had been Bests in her day, she would have been num-ber one. Riya was famous for being the godmother who stood by the clever and fearless Princess Savitri. Fawn opened her Wish List to Savitri's page, but she didn't really need to. Isabelle knew her story by heart. When Riya became

Princess Savitri's godmother, Savitri was grown up, married, and mostly happily ever after. But then tragedy struck. Her husband grew ill. So Savitri asked Riya for the strength and determination to stand up to Fate and save him from death. Although that seemed impossible, Savitri (with Riya's help) tricked the gods. The princess and her husband remained happily ever after.

Not many princesses attempted to mess with destiny this way. Not many godmothers would say yes to helping. But Riya did. She risked it all.

And now she was here, and she was cheering on Minerva against Grandmomma! Isabelle stayed in the tree. When Grandmomma and Luciana (but not Clotilda) arrived with their own megaphones and loaded wands, she hoped that this would all be over soon.

Grandmomma turned on her sparkly megaphone. (She knew what she was doing.) First, she At first, it made a terrible squeaky sound. But when it was working, she said, "We are here to listen."

Isabelle peered through the leaves and petals. Listening was good. Listening meant progress.

Now it was Minerva's turn. She moved her soapbox closer to Grandmomma. She climbed onto it so she could (almost) look Grandmomma in the eye. Isabelle crossed her fingers and hoped Minerva would say something polite. But instead, she stamped her foot. She shouted into her plain (but not squeaky) megaphone, "Have you read our manifesto?"

All the godmothers behind her waved their copies above their heads.

Grandmomma spoke slowly. "I will be happy to read your manifesto, and consider all your points. But first I ask you to do one thing for me: Remove the name W.A.R."

It was not a lot to ask.

Or maybe it was.

Because Minerva said no. "I'm sorry. But we can't."

The godmothers behind her jeered. A few yelled, "Sparkly and bitter," and, "You need to retire."

Kaminari, Raine, and Luciana stood by Grandmomma's side. Luciana said, "In the spirit of compromise and fairness, one word is not a big concession."

But Minerva wouldn't budge. "So let me get this straight: It's okay that you call us Worsts. But we can't use the word *war*?"

Isabelle thought they were both being stubborn. She shouted, "Read the manifesto already," and, "You don't believe in war either."

But nobody heard her. They were all staring at Zahara.

She picked up her megaphone. "Mothers, we are not going to change anything until our ideas are heard. Are you with me?"

"Nobody is a Worst," the crowd chanted.

"We are at W.A.R.!" Minerva shouted.

"Sparkly but bitter!" Zahara yelled.

Grandmomma pointed her finger (the one not holding her wand) at her old friend. "You never could stay out of trouble."

This should have scared Zahara, but it didn't. "My friend," she said, "this is on you. You always thought you knew more than everyone else. Ever since you chose to send away your own daughter. But you never listen."

At the mention of Mom, everyone stopped shouting. Grandmomma took five steps backward. Raine and Kaminari ushered her over to the READY door of the center and huddled around her.

Talking about Mom made the Bests uncomfortable—but not Luciana.

She did not back up. Instead, she flicked her wand and turned the entire sky red. "Fine," she said. "Make your signs. Have your strike. March as much as you want."

Before she could say or do anything else, Isabelle, followed by Angelica and Fawn, jumped out of the gnarly tree.

"Grandmomma! What is Zahara talking about?" Isabelle asked.

"And what about training?" Angelica asked Luciana.

"Lo siento," Luciana said, "but you know the rules. Why don't you go back to the castle? Make yourselves some nice snacks. In a little while, Clotilda will go over what will happen next."

When she swirled her wand, the air turned cold. (She knew this would annoy the Worsts.) Then she made the clouds grow dark. It felt like a storm was coming.

Isabelle, however, was not going anywhere—not until someone answered her question. She marched through the crowd to Zahara and Minerva. "What do you mean she chose to send her away? I thought my mother had to go. What do you know?"

Chapter Eleven

The Very Short and Sad Story of the Unhappy Princess, as Told by Zahara

Warning: This remains a very sad story. It is the story of a very unhappy princess and her fairy godmother, Isabelle's mother. No matter how much we want it to end differently, it will always end the same way—unhappily ever after. (If you want to see Clotilda's version, see *The Wish List #1: The Worst Fairy Godmother Ever.* She blames the princess for wanting too much. If you think it was the fairy godmother's fault, you'll probably prefer Angelica's version, in *The Wish List #2: Keep Calm and Sparkle On!*)

Zahara kept it brief—since all the Worsts knew her version by heart. Also: She didn't have a ton of energy. She was an ancient godmother carrying a heavy sign. This whole strike thing was wearing her out.

"Once upon a time, your mother became an official fairy godmother. Her first princess was a spoiled one. She spent too much time looking in the mirror.

"Your mother did what she could. And for a while, that princess was beloved. But it was never going to work out. That's because there were powerful godmothers who wanted to change the rules.

"When the princess grew unhappy, they decided that this was their opportunity. They made a big fuss. They acted like the regular world would never recover. Your grandmother sent your mother away. They used her to make a bunch of rules and that's why we're here today."

Zahara dropped her wand.

Grandmomma put her hands on Isabelle's shoulders. "I'm sorry, Isabelle. So very, very sorry."

Isabelle felt like kicking something. "You mean this is true?"

Grandmomma's shoulders slumped. The lines in her face seemed deeper. "She makes it sound so simple, but it wasn't like that at all."

This was not really an answer to her question.

Instead, Grandmomma told them what would happen now that the strike had begun. "I'm so sorry to tell you that I will not cross their picket line. So I must regretfully tell you that I'm canceling Level Three for this season." She explained that somewhere in the bylaws of the Official Fairy Godmother Association was a section about respecting differing opinions and that, in order to be fair, they needed to resolve the strike before any business could continue.

As a small consolation—or perhaps to get her young charges out of there—she handed each of them a small velvet pouch containing one multicolored sparkle each. "If we can resolve things in time to resume, we will. If not, we'll be in touch."

Then she walked away.

There was nothing else to say.

Chapter Twelve

The Science of Sparkles

$\mathcal{A}$ngelica and Fawn did not want to insert their sparkles into their wands. They didn't want to leave. "So this is it? We don't get to learn anything?"

Obviously, the strike was the worst news ever. Not just because they couldn't wait to learn the science of sparkles. They were also worried about Nora and the ring. So they ran back down the path past the trees and the fields, back to the castle. They were prepared to tell Clotilda everything—if they had to.

She was sitting on the steps of the castle. Sulking.

"Your grandmomma should have banished Minerva when she had the chance," Angelica said.

"I didn't think it was possible to feel sparkly and bitter at the same time," Fawn said.

Clotilda agreed with Fawn. "Sparkly and frustrated, for sure. And maybe even sparkly and confused. But sparkly and bitter? She's just saying that to get on Grandmomma's nerves."

"How long do you think this will last?" Isabelle asked.

Clotilda hoped the Bests and Worsts settled their differences soon. "How am I going to explain to Roxanne that she has to be patient? That I can't grant any wishes? She's difficult on a good day. But if I can't help her, she's going to be impossible."

It was almost a relief to hear her sister complain about normal fairy godmother problems. "What do you mean—impossible? I thought you said you were up for a challenge."

"Roxanne can't decide what she wants." Clotilda took out her Wish List to show them the record of their interactions. "One day, she says she'll be happy if she becomes the mayor. Then the next day, she wants to provide books for every single school in the world or food for someone or a house. Or get everyone into college. The non-wishes just don't end. You'd almost think she didn't want a fairy godmother. It's like she thinks that being a modern princess means you have to do everything yourself!"

Angelica assured her she'd figure it out—she thought Clotilda was destined for greatness. "You can do anything. Even without sparkles."

"But what about me?" Isabelle asked. "Without time to practice, I'm going to forget everything! My wand work will grow rusty." She sighed. "I'll never be as good as you."

This was true. But she was flattering Clotilda for a reason, too.

Isabelle wanted to convince Clotilda to take them back to the basement and teach them some science so they could get back to Nora. (She also wanted to look for the box—the one that said DO NOT TOUCH.)

Clotilda was not going to be duped again. "I'm sorry," she said, "but no means no. Even if I wanted to, my hands and wand are tied. Magic is not allowed. I know this is hard, but you're going to have to be patient."

Being patient was the same thing as waiting. "It's so not fair. Why can't you show us what we were going to learn in class?" When Clotilda shook her head, Isabelle tried a different tactic. "Would you rather I tell Grandmomma that you gave me an orange sparkle?"

Clotilda frowned.

"Or that you took us to the basement?"

Angelica and Fawn nodded. "Or that you let us touch those wands?"

Clotilda stamped her foot. "You wouldn't!"

"We would."

Clotilda paced. She kicked the stoop. She did not enjoy breaking rules. She hadn't expected Isabelle to play dirty.

"Okay," she said. "I'll teach you one lesson. But that's it! And nobody breathes a word. Are all of you clear?"

Quickly (before she changed her mind), they donned their protective gear and walked as carefully as they could (all things considered) down the dark spiral staircase.

At the bottom, Clotilda set up a large table, perfect for learning the science of sparkles. She also made a couple of lamps so they could see what they were doing, and a fan to suck up any extra fumes.

Then she set up three separate workstations, complete with a square-shaped beaker with a lid, a tray, and something called a colorimeter. Fawn was very excited about that. "It figures out how much pure magic is in a sparkle! Kaminari told me all about it. She said they can help you make your magic more accurate."

Clotilda pulled two vials of sparkles out of her box. One was pure red. The other was pure blue.

"What about yellow?" Angelica asked.

"What about it?" Clotilda looked like she was about to make everything (including them) disappear. So none of them pushed it. Instead, they let her talk.

"The first step to good science is understanding your materials, your tools, and your environment." She waved her wand, and four pairs of tweezers appeared. A light shone on the tabletop. The temperature got cooler. "The second step is to know your sparkles." She paused. "Who remembers what red and blue are for?"

Angelica and Fawn raised their hands. Isabelle didn't. (She was looking for the box.) But she knew the answer: "Red is for girl power. And blue is for loyalty."

Clotilda gave Isabelle a thumbs-up. "And when you put them together, then you make . . ."

Isabelle said nothing this time (still looking). But Fawn and Angelica knew the answer. "Purple. For trust!"

Clotilda handed them each a pair of clean tweezers. "The reason we teach trust first is that it can have many uses.

Pure purple offers your princess wisdom. She'll be able to step back and see things with more patience."

Isabelle thought she spied the box. (It was under the stairs.) *Can you get on with it?* she thought. She had a plan. It did not include more waiting.

Clotilda told them to stand back.

She opened her sparkle tray and picked up a single red sparkle and a single blue sparkle. She put each one on a separate "slide," or piece of what looked like glass—to confirm that the sparkles were equal in weight. Then she placed each sparkle, one at a time, in the colorimeter.

The red was 100 percent pure red. The blue was 100 percent pure blue. They weighed exactly the same.

"Perfect," she said. "Now you do it."

They each measured and weighed their sparkles.

"Now put them in your beakers and make sure the lid is tight," Clotilda said.

"Why does it have to be tight?" Isabelle asked.

"Because you don't want any of the magic to escape."

When nothing much happened, Clotilda wondered if it might be too cold in the basement. "Jiggle your beakers," she said. "Vigorously, but not too vigorously."

First, Fawn's beaker filled with smoke. A second later, so did Angelica's.

Isabelle picked up her beaker and gave it a quick shake. The sparkles shifted around a lot, but nothing else happened.

"Why are you so timid? I said, give it a jiggle."

When Isabelle's sparkles still wouldn't smoke, Clotilda put her hands on top of Isabelle's and shook the beaker hard. That worked.

"Now sit back," Clotilda said. "And be prepared to be amazed."

So they sat there until the smoke in the beakers cleared to reveal three perfect purple sparkles.

"We did it!" Isabelle said. She reached for the lid of her beaker, but Clotilda swatted her with her wand. "Isabelle! Back off! They need to cool down!"

When they had waited for what seemed to Isabelle like an hour (but was probably more like five minutes), Clotilda removed the lids and gathered up the sparkles. While she measured them in the colorimeter, Isabelle got her friends' attention. She motioned toward the box.

(When a box is marked DO NOT TOUCH, you don't have to explain why you want to steal it.)

Isabelle needed two extra seconds for her secret plan. "Before we go, can we look at the frogs? Just to say hi?"

"The frogs? Again?" Clotilda asked. She was out of patience. She also underestimated her sister. (She thought she hid that box well.)

As Angelica and Fawn said hi to Cornelius as well as to a young frog named Bert, Isabelle grabbed the box from under the stairs and stuffed it beneath her protective gear.

This was not that difficult since the box was small and not heavy. Also: Three heads are better than one.

When they got back upstairs, Isabelle hid the box in the bin with their protective gear while Angelica and Fawn distracted Clotilda the best way they knew how—with gratitude and flattery. They used lines ranging from "Thank you so much" to "We will always be grateful" to "Roxanne is the luckiest princess in the entire world to have a wonderful, perfect, delightful fairy godmother like you."

(This might have alerted another fairy godmother, but flattery was Clotilda's weak spot.)

Now all they had to do was wait.

It didn't take a long time. Clotilda was sick of babysitting the trainees. She also didn't want to do them any more favors.

As soon as she was gone, Fawn did a little happy dance. Angelica opened the bin and pulled out the box. "That was brilliant!" she told Isabelle. "You are so sneaky."

"What do you think is in the box?"

"I don't know, but I want to find out. Let's go to the girlgoyles. Whatever is in it, we don't want to be caught."

Chapter Thirteen

How to Break the Rules without Really Breaking Them

The spot between the girlgoyles was safe, but it was also a very tight fit.

To make enough room, Fawn had to lean on the girlgoyle on the left. Angelica hugged the girlgoyle on the right. She was so giddy from the science of sparkles, she put a (stolen) pair of goggles on the helpless girlgoyle and asked her, "What do you think is in the box?"

Of course, the girlgoyles said nothing. They didn't laugh at the jokes. Or worry about the contents of a box.

(This was the problem with friends made of rock.)

Isabelle, standing in the middle, tried to open the box in the traditional way—by pulling on the tape. But no matter how hard she pulled, the wrapping held together. It was sealed with magic. Therefore, they needed magic to open it.

The only magic they had were the single solitary sparkles that Grandmomma had given them when she canceled Level Three training. Fawn said, "If we all aim our wands at one spot, we should have enough power to open any box."

"And what if we can't?" Angelica asked. "Or even worse, what if we open the box and it's empty inside?"

If they used their sparkles to open an empty box, they would have nothing to do for the rest of the strike. But none of them believed a box marked DO NOT TOUCH could be empty; this was a risk they were willing to take.

As they loaded their wands, Isabelle said, "We'll do it on three. One, two . . ."

"Stop!" Angelica said. "Isabelle, your glasses!" (They were on top of Isabelle's head.)

Isabelle slipped them on. Then she apologized. (Her wand was nowhere near the box.) "Can we take it from the top?"

Fawn offered a suggestion. "We might have even more power if we all focus our sparkles on our best birthday memories ever."

Isabelle lowered her wand. "The best what?"

"Our best birthdays. To increase the odds of getting that lid open." She said, "Our magic isn't that powerful, but if we combine our sparkles with good memories, we will definitely succeed." Angelica agreed that this was a great idea. She nodded—she had chosen a memory. Fawn did the same thing. (She really was a superior fairy godmother trainee.)

Isabelle remembered a birthday long ago. Grandmomma was sitting in a comfy chair. Clotilda was handing her a gift. They were all laughing and celebrating and relaxing. Because there was someone else there. Someone sparkly. Full of yellow and green and blue and every other color.

BOOM!

The top of the box burst open. A lot of blue, red, and yellow dust flew into the air.

When it cleared, the trainees looked inside.

Inside the box were four things: a broken wand, a pair of goggles monogrammed with the letter *V*, an old dusty beaker (with matching lid), and best of all, a small glittery pouch. Inside the pouch were some smaller bags full of mostly pink and multicolored sparkles. But also some red, yellow, orange, and gray.

Isabelle picked up the goggles. Then she put them down. *V* could stand for Victoria. (That was her mother's name.)

Fawn gave Isabelle a quick hug. (She knew what *V* stood for, too.) "Maybe we should give this stuff to Clotilda." If it belonged to Isabelle's mom, it could be dangerous.

There was no way Isabelle wanted to tell Clotilda.

Angelica agreed. "Did you accidentally touch a yellow sparkle?" she asked Fawn. "Look at all these sparkles! This is our chance to have an adventure!"

"And check on Nora," Isabelle added.

With that decided, they went inside and opened up the book to the *Official Guide to the Spectrum of Sparkles* to make sure they knew what each sparkle could do.

Not all the colors matched perfectly, but they seemed close enough. They divided them into three equal portions.

"Now what do we do?" Angelica asked. But she meant, "What can we get away with?"

They couldn't help a princess.

They couldn't help a regular girl.

They couldn't tell anyone or ask for help or in any way risk getting caught by the Bests.

They needed a plan.

"We could start by practicing on your girlgoyles," Angelica suggested.

"Absolutely not," Isabelle said. The girlgoyles might be made of rock, but up until recently, they were the only friends she had. She didn't want anything bad to happen to them.

One last time, they reviewed everything they'd learned. And everything they'd read. And everything they'd seen in the basement.

But each and every time, they hit a dead end.

Isabelle felt awful. She hoped Nora was having a good time at the tournament. And that the orange sparkle hadn't made her do anything too silly. And that she was on the same team as Mason.

That gave Isabelle an idea. "Is there anything in the Wish List about boys?"

"Where are we going to meet boys?" Fawn asked.

"Don't you remember? At Nora's camp." Isabelle was very excited. "What if we find Mason and his friends and answer their wishes? That won't go in the Wish List. We can practice all we want!" (It meant she could also check on Nora! Without bugging them about it.)

Since Isabelle wasn't exactly the most reliable student, Angelica and Fawn frantically paged through the second half of their rule book. (Because they weren't ready to even think about love, they hadn't gotten to any of the sections that concerned boys.)

As they searched, Isabelle looked out over the fairy godmother world. Helping boys would definitely be a challenge. So far, she'd only met two: Gregory, Nora's little brother, and Mason, who hung out with Samantha and Nora. During Level Two, he liked being in the play but had no interest in kissing.

She couldn't believe how long it was taking Angelica and Fawn to page through their books. "Isn't there an index—or a table of contents? Or some quick tool to look up *things about boys*?"

Fawn gave her the stink eye. "There is an index, Isabelle. But the books are fat. And unless I'm missing something, you're not helping."

So they went inside to get Isabelle's book. They sat on her bed. They read a little bit longer, but soon, all three trainees were satisfied.

"The Wish List doesn't even mention boys," Angelica declared.

"I think they're fair game," Fawn said. "How different could they be?"

Angelica had lots of questions. "How do we approach them? How will we know which boys deserve wishes? What if we can't grant their wishes? What do we say?"

These were not foolish questions. Angelica and Fawn had worked only with practice princesses—girls who had already made wishes.

Isabelle was now the expert. "First of all, you have to be patient, since they haven't wished and don't know you're coming. So don't whip out your wand too fast. Once they believe, they'll want all kinds of things. Both Nora and

Samantha wished for more wishes. I bet regular boys are exactly the same."

The truth was, Isabelle didn't care how she got her friends to say yes. She only cared about seeing Nora. She had to make sure she was okay.

Fawn and Angelica knew this. "Can we trust you around Nora?" Angelica asked.

"You'll have to," Isabelle said. "Just like I'll have to trust you."

When they were all ready, the trainees gathered around the girlgoyles and pointed their wands high in the air. They imagined Nora's camp, and together they flung their sparkles into the sky.

This time, Nora was not singing. She was muttering to herself. It sounded like she was hiding.

Chapter Fourteen

Still Serious Nora

When three fairy godmothers (who look like regular girls, but still) appear out of thin air in the woods, they will always scare a regular girl—especially when that regular girl is lonely and all alone and wanting her problems to disappear (in the regular, un-magical way, of course).

In other words, when Nora saw them, she screamed. Then Isabelle screamed. Then Fawn and Angelica screamed—not because they were scared but because everyone else was screaming and the whole thing was confusing. They ran in circles and got very excited and Angelica and Fawn might have dropped all their sparkles, but they were able to step back and get control of themselves.

"Why are you all alone in the woods?" Isabelle asked Nora.

"I'm hiding. Because everyone hates me." Nora pulled a bright-red bandanna out of her pocket and held it tightly. "Whose team are you on?"

Isabelle remembered that there were four colors. "I'm on green, and they're on gold." When Nora still looked suspicious (because Angelica was wearing red), Isabelle said, "We're not having the best time either. Why do you think everyone hates you?"

Nora stuffed her flag deep in her pocket—just in case. "Haven't you heard? After I met you, I felt brave. I tried to make friends. But it didn't go well."

Isabelle felt for the ring in her pocket. "What happened?"

"Well, when one of the girls started talking about soccer, I didn't have anything to add, so I suggested that we all do a project instead. I had a ton of ideas." She shrugged. "I might have gotten a little too enthusiastic."

That didn't seem that bad. Or surprising. "And then?"

"I suggested cleaning up the pond."

Isabelle couldn't help laughing. Nora was like a regular girl and a fairy godmother wrapped up in one.

"I told them that Mason and I had done lots of projects, and then everything changed. Because they wanted to talk about Mason. Especially one girl. She had a million questions." She shook her head. "When I told her I knew Mason really well, she asked me if I liked Mason—and when I said *of course I did*, the girl got mad. She thought that meant I liked-liked him, and before I could correct her, they all started singing and making fun of me."

"That doesn't sound so bad," Fawn said.

But Nora wasn't finished. "When they wouldn't stop, I got upset. I told them that the tournament was stupid. And that they were stupid for caring so much about a game when there were really important things to care about."

Okay. This was bad.

Nora looked down at the ground. "Now no one wants to have anything to do with me. They moved my cot next to the bathroom. And this morning, I was the last person picked for the Red Team!"

Isabelle didn't know what it was like to sleep next to the bathroom, but she did know what it was like to feel lonely—and to make a mistake and not be able to take it back. She knew Nora, too, and even though Nora cared a lot about the world, she also liked having friends. And playing games.

This didn't sound like Nora.

It didn't sound like orange, either.

Nora continued. "The worst part is that last night, they stayed up telling stories. Then they snuck out for a midnight walk. But they didn't invite me to come along." She picked up a stick and threw it as hard as she could—not very far. "So today, I'm hiding. And I'm going to keep hiding," she said, kicking a stone, "until my dad gets my card and takes me home."

Isabelle flinched. (The word *home* was almost as powerful as *wish*.)

Nora flinched, too, but for a different reason. In the distance, a loud, low horn blew. "The ram's horn," she said. "That means one game is ending and another is beginning. People might be walking nearby. I have to go."

As Nora took off, Isabelle reached for her wand. But Angelica stopped her. "Unless you can control yourself around Nora, we have to go back!" She added (a little nicer), "We know this is hard, but this is her problem. There is nothing we can do to help her."

Isabelle put away her wand. She promised she could restrain herself. She wouldn't grant wishes or use any magic or do anything to get them into trouble.

She knew they were here to practice on boys.

They didn't want to get caught.

But that didn't mean she couldn't help in a non-magical way.

She was Nora's fairy godmother. Even without magic, happily ever after had to be a possibility.

Chapter Fifteen

Boy Problems

By the time the trainees walked out of the woods and around a pond, there were soccer games happening on two adjacent fields. Red versus Green. And Blue versus Gold.

Angelica tightened her glittery purple sneakers. She pointed to an older girl in a red T-shirt, running up and down the field, blowing her whistle, and shouting directions. "She looks a little like a young Galina," Fawn said. "Where's Mason?"

Angelica pointed to a kid sitting on the edge of the bench. (He looked miserable.) "That's not him, is it?"

"No," Isabelle said, scanning the field. "He's the one with floppy hair and the yellow cap and the bright yellow T-shirt." On his T-shirt, he'd written TEAM GREEN. Unlike everyone else on the field, he wasn't chasing the ball. Instead, he was sort of jogging in place near the net.

Isabelle wondered if he didn't like playing soccer, but when a tall boy in a red shirt kicked the ball to Mason's end of the field, he was ready. He kicked the ball to one of his friends, and it looked like a good move. But then a girl in a bright red T-shirt and bandanna around her head sprinted forward and intercepted a pass. She kicked the ball right past Mason's friend (and another boy) into the net.

Half the kids on the field groaned.

Half cheered.

Mason kicked the ground and then looked up at the sky (the way you do when you are mad at your friend but don't want to say anything). When each team scored again, an older boy in a green shirt told Mason and a couple of others to sit down and take a break.

Mason sat by himself. He leaned against a big tree.

This was their chance!

Isabelle, Angelica, and Fawn made a plan. "You talk to him," they said to Isabelle. "We'll hide on the other side of the tree. When he tells you what he wants, we'll load up our wands."

It seemed simple enough, so Isabelle went over and sat down next to Mason. "Tough break," she said.

"We're all tired from Capture the Flag," he said. "Plus the Blue Team won in a landslide! No matter what happens, I don't think any team can catch up now."

Isabelle wasn't here to talk sports. "Isn't your name Mason? You're Nora's friend, right?"

"Is she here?" He looked around. "Everyone keeps asking me if I like her–like her. Don't ask me why."

Isabelle told him what happened. "But don't be mad! I don't think she doesn't like you. She just doesn't . . . you know."

"Phew," Mason said. "That's a relief." (He'd had enough of girls who liked him–liked him.) "If you see her," he said, standing up and walking toward the sideline, "tell her to come back and play. Tell her that nobody's mad—that whatever happened, it's probably already over. When the tournament is on, everyone just wants to have fun."

Isabelle hoped that was true. She was about to tell Mason more, but then she felt a hard jab in her side. It was Angelica. (She had sharp, long nails.)

"Hurry up," she whispered, "and ask him what he wants. Or else! We want to try out these sparkles!"

Since she couldn't ask what "or else" meant, she followed Mason to the sideline. "If you could wish for anything, what would it be?"

Mason looked at her strangely. "I don't know," he said. "I guess, wish me luck. You see that girl Ella?" He pointed to a girl in a bright red shirt and bandanna. "She's amazing. I don't want her getting past me again."

"Good luck," Isabelle said as he ran out onto the field. Then she ran back to the tree. "You heard that, right?"

Angelica was ready. With a flick and a twist, she hit him square in the back with a single multicolor sparkle.

The magic was immediate.

First, Mason charged the ball—more like a bull than a boy. He kicked it so hard it whipped past the other players, past the net, and hit a tree. Then it fell to the ground, deflated.

That was just the beginning.

From there, Mason ran between both fields, kicking ball after ball until all of them had popped. When everyone stopped playing (because all the balls were gone), he started running in circles—like he couldn't stop.

"Something has gone wrong," Isabelle said. "Look at the sky."

As Mason ran in circles, the clouds followed him. The birds overhead looked strange, too. They were flying backward.

This was not good.

"How strong was that sparkle?" Fawn asked.

"It looked like the weakest sparkle in the bag," Angelica said, shaking any remaining sparkle out of her wand. "I didn't think it would even do anything."

This gave Fawn an idea. She loaded her wand with a couple of red sparkles and flicked them toward Mason. Mason stopped running, and Isabelle felt a glimmer of hope. But then he broke into song and twirled like a dancer, around and around and around and around. And if that wasn't embarrassing enough, he dropped to the ground, got down on one knee right in front of Ella, and began to recite poetry.

The trainees didn't know what to do. As Mason's poetry got mushier and mushier, they scrambled to find a better sparkle. They hit him with blue, then red, then yellow. But he didn't stop.

At first, Ella seemed happy. Maybe even happily ever after. But then she turned around and saw that everyone was laughing. So Fawn flicked Mason with a shiny black sparkle.

For a moment, the trainees were pretty sure this had worked.

He got off his knee, and stopped talking. Then he bowed toward the crowd that had assembled.

And then—to everyone's surprise—he put his hands on the ground and kicked like a donkey. He yelled, "Hee-haw!" And he wouldn't stop. Even when Ella ran away.

This was a disaster.

All they had wanted to do was practice! And now no one was happy! Not Nora! Not Mason! Not anybody!

Angelica wanted to return to the fairy godmother world for help, but Fawn didn't think it was right to leave Mason like this. She didn't know how long the magic would last. She also didn't want to get in trouble.

In frustration, she turned on Isabelle. "I can't believe we trusted you. You're the daughter of the worst fairy god-mother ever! What did we expect?"

Chapter Sixteen

More Boy Problems, or Nowhere Near Happily Ever After

That was mean. It was also unfair. "I'm sorry," Fawn said.

"So am I," said Angelica. "We dared you to come. This is our fault, too."

While the trainees promised to be nicer to each other, Mason recited a new poem. He also continued to bray and kick. A few kids took pictures. He looked really miserable and confused.

But he also couldn't stop.

Isabelle took out some sparkles. She told Angelica and Fawn, "There has to be something we can do—something we're missing. I'm not giving up."

First, she chucked a yellow sparkle. Then she flicked a pale green one. When Ella left the field with her friends, Angelica and Fawn reloaded their wands.

"Maybe we're going at this the wrong way," Fawn said. "Maybe boys aren't like girls. Maybe they're the opposites." She loaded the bright orange sparkles into her wand and whipped her wand hard in Mason's direction.

This was an excellent theory, but now they had a new problem: There were too many kids in the way. Just as the sparkles were about to hit Mason square in the jaw, a bunch of boys stepped in front of him. So the magic hit them instead.

It didn't take long for them to start acting strange, too.

First they started tumbling on the ground. Then they grabbed partners and started waltzing around the field in a great big circle.

Isabelle couldn't help laughing. They looked ridiculous! But Fawn was not amused. "We have to get them to stop." She paused. "Think peaceful, quiet thoughts. Slow thoughts. Thoughtful thoughts. We need to calm them down."

Isabelle thought about mornings. And big breakfasts. And the way the fairy godmother world looked from the spot between the girlgoyles. When nothing happened, she thought about breakfast in bed. And sunshine. And rain. And when that didn't work either, Fawn said, "Aha!" She loaded her wand and showered the field with pink.

It looked a little bit like snow.

Isabelle asked, "Do you even know what pink does?"

"Normally, humor," Fawn said. "In this case, I think it will calm everyone down."

Fortunately, she was right.

Mason stopped reciting and kicking. The waltzing boys stopped dancing. And one boy who couldn't stop giggling finally quieted down.

The tournament captains blew their whistles. "Okay, that's enough with the silliness." They sent some boys onto the field. And some back to the bench. Then the Red Team captain caught Angelica's eye. "You! In the bright red shirt! Go in for Nora—wherever she is!"

Isabelle and Fawn watched Angelica take over the game. She was fast. She was accurate. She saved three goals in five minutes. (She was just as good as Ella.)

Isabelle couldn't believe her eyes when she noticed Fawn following a group of boys from the Gold Team. "Where are you going now?"

"To the art shack. With those boys," Fawn said. "I want to see what happens when everyone isn't running around. Maybe the problem isn't the sparkles. Maybe it's soccer." She told Isabelle that the boys had to help paint a mural for the Tournament of Champions.

(Apparently, each team had to make one.)

She loaded her wand. "Don't worry. I promise I'll be careful."

But it's hard to keep this type of promise when sparkles are involved.

In this case, every single boy grabbed some paint and some brushes and splattered the mural with dots of wet paint. Then they splattered themselves with wet paint. And then they stomped and rolled on the mural. And then they tore it to bits.

The art captain couldn't stop blowing her whistle. "What are you doing? Why are you destroying your mural?"

She sent them all to their bunks so they could think about what had gone wrong. "You'll be the only team without one," she said.

The boys, of course, couldn't explain what was happening. They were just as confused as the art captain was!

Isabelle told Fawn, "Let's go back to the field and find Angelica. We have to stop." And for once, Fawn totally agreed.

Magic was in the air, but the sparkles weren't working. There was something going on that they didn't understand.

Isabelle sat down under a tree. She wished she could find Nora—not to do magic. Just to say good-bye. And also apologize. And tell her that she didn't need to worry about stinking at soccer—that every single boy looked silly on the field. And Ella probably didn't care about Mason (that way) anymore.

She pulled the ring out of her pocket and prepared to throw it as hard as she could so she would never see it again. But then she noticed that the yellow had changed. Now the ring was all green. Green meant responsibility. Integrity. And leadership.

Was the ring playing jokes on her? No matter which version of her mom's story she believed, her mom hadn't had any of those qualities.

And neither did Isabelle.

Isabelle's stomach turned. She began to sweat. After all that studying with Grandmomma, she had done every single thing wrong. She shouldn't have come to camp. Or agreed to use sparkles. She could have stood up for

Minerva, Irene, and MaryEllen—but she hadn't done that, either.

"Let's go home," Isabelle said. "Magic is supposed to be fun. We're supposed to make girls happily ever after. I'll take the blame. I'm the one who stole the box of sparkles."

Angelica and Fawn felt terrible about everything, too. "This is not all your fault," Angelica said. "We dared you to come here."

"We wanted to practice, too," Fawn said. She gathered up the rest of the sparkles and put them in one bag. "Can we just throw these away? Is that safe?"

"No, it isn't," a familiar voice said.

Before Isabelle could turn around, she felt a cold hand on her shoulder. This hand was not bony. It was soft. And smooth.

Clotilda! It was almost a relief to see her sister. "What are you doing here?" Isabelle asked. "How did you find us?"

Clotilda didn't answer. "Let's go," she told the trainees. "All of you have a lot of explaining to do."

Chapter Seventeen

The Inevitable Chapter When Isabelle Gets Help from Clotilda

Four flicks and a sparkle later, the trainees arrived at Clotilda's room. Angelica and Fawn could not stop themselves from examining every corner of the room. They loved Clotilda's pictures and her furniture and her neatly made bed and all her not-ever-bitter sparkles.

They started to compliment her taste in everything, but unfortunately, flattery wasn't going to work anymore. Clotilda was furious. "Hand them over," she said. "And I mean all of them. Now."

Without any argument at all, the trainees gave her the rest of their sparkles. They tried to look sorry. And sweet. (They all knew a lecture was coming.)

"I am so disappointed in all of you. When you asked me to take you to the basement, I trusted you and treated you like real godmothers."

Isabelle raised her hand before Clotilda could scold them much longer. "The sparkles were mine. I suggested we go and see Nora." She added, "I had this feeling she needed me."

"That's not the whole story," Fawn said, linking her arm in Isabelle's. "Angelica and I dared you to take us to Nora. We used those sparkles together."

Angelica looked really mad—at Clotilda. "For the record, don't pretend you trusted us." She reminded everyone they'd needed to use threats—not trust—to get Clotilda to take them to the basement.

Clotilda looked a little uncomfortable. But also proud. The trainees might be in trouble, but they were friends. They stood together.

Isabelle could tell her sister felt conflicted. "We feel so bad. We had no idea that doing magic on boys could cause so many problems." If flattery didn't work, maybe honesty would. And humility.

Together, they opened the velvet bag and poured out all their sparkles. Clotilda put each one in her colorimeter. Every time, the sparkles came up corrupted. The red were only 65 percent red. And the blue were 81 percent green.

"What you have here are some very stale, out-of-date sparkles." Clotilda pointed her wand at the whole pile. She said, "Say good-bye," and *pop, pop, pop, zing!* They disappeared.

She looked more serious than Nora. "For your information," she began, "sparkles have an expiration date. They must be stored properly. And all of you should have known that, because we never mix colors in one bag." When they all nodded in understanding, she continued, "Even if you knew what effect fresh sparkles might have on boys, you had no idea what old, lousy sparkles would do." She paced around her room. "Where did you even get these? From the Worsts?"

Before Isabelle could confess, Fawn said, "We found them. We didn't know how long it takes for sparkles to go stale. Honestly, we were just trying to get in some practice."

A look of concern passed over Clotilda's face. "Found them? Where?"

Isabelle, Fawn, and Angelica stared at the ground.

Clotilda was not happy. "This is really important. Either someone isn't storing sparkles safely, or she is practicing bad sparkle science."

"Bad sparkle science?"

Clotilda explained "Why do you think the Bests regulate sparkles? Why do you think we created all the levels? The spectrum? The colorimeters?"

She told them to take out their notebooks so they'd never forget what she was about to say. "When you work with sparkles, you must control for many variables, from purity to expiration, to the particular ratios you have added to your beaker. This is important because each color has a specific purpose. The Bests and other godmothers spend a great deal of time making sure that every single sparkle is pure, premeasured, and tested before it is used to help make princesses happily ever after. When you use a spoiled, expired, or unmeasured sparkle, you can't predict or control what happens."

Isabelle found this extremely interesting. "But if they were old, why did they cause so much chaos? Was it all because we used sparkles on boys?"

Clotilda sighed. "It's because aged sparkles like these are unpredictable. They look dull—because they weren't vacuum-sealed. If you had brought them to me, I would have told you that these sparkles wouldn't work. Or even worse, they could be tainted with bad magic." Clotilda wagged her finger. "But you didn't. So you didn't know."

After the trainees apologized (again) and made all sorts of promises (also again), Clotilda had had enough. "I know this strike is a bummer, but you need to have more patience.

You'll learn all the sparkle science you could ever want to know soon enough. Then, once we know that you understand how to manage the basics, we'll let you experiment a little more."

Isabelle hugged her sister. "We totally get it. But that still doesn't explain the ring—"

Clotilda held up her hand to interrupt Isabelle. "What ring?"

Isabelle pulled it out of her pocket. "The ring you left me on the girlgoyles—that belonged to Mom. Nora had one just like it." When Clotilda looked shocked, Isabelle said, "You did leave it. Didn't you?"

"I didn't leave you anything." Clotilda grabbed the ring from Isabelle and examined it. "How long have you been wearing this?" Clotilda asked. "Why did you let Nora try it on? Especially if you thought it belonged to our mom?"

"She was so unhappy," Isabelle said. "And her ring looked similar—but not magic, of course." She told Clotilda everything that happened: How she'd found the ring. How the ring had started out yellow and green, until Nora put it on and it turned bright orange. "It made her say things she didn't want to say. And then, after a while, it turned completely green."

That's what it was now. A pure and perfect green.

"Why is it changing color?" Angelica asked. "Do you know?"

Clotilda looked at Isabelle in a new way. (Less annoyed and more impressed.) "Do you remember what green stands for?"

Angelica raised her hand. "It's from the integrity family. So it means responsibility. And compromise."

Clotilda nodded. "In other words . . . leadership."

Isabelle laughed. "But I'm not a leader. And neither was Mom. And why did it turn orange when Nora put it on?"

Clotilda told her that rings like this were not made of sparkles—that they had no real magic. "They're just old trinkets that godmothers used to give their princesses—for fun." She explained, "When Nora put it on, the ring showed you—not her—that she needed confidence. That she was feeling low. And scared. If you had been her official fairy godmother, you would have known how to help."

"But she said she felt different after putting it on," Isabelle said.

Clotilda smiled. "That was your doing. You must have given her some confidence—with your heart. Not the ring."

Fawn and Angelica agreed. "She knew just what to say," Fawn said. "You can tell Isabelle is going to be a great fairy godmother."

That was a nice thing to hear, but it didn't fix the situation. "This is so unfair! If we had left Nora alone, she might have made friends. She wouldn't be sleeping near the bathroom. She'd be having fun at the tournament, celebrating her birthday."

Clotilda said, "You can't stop princesses from making mistakes." She put her arm around her sister. "Besides, it's not the mistake that defines her—or any of us. When it comes to character, it's how we get out of our mistakes that matters."

(That was profound.)

But Isabelle had a feeling she wasn't talking just about Nora, either. "What are you saying?"

Clotilda smiled. "I'm saying that the yellow is gone. The ring is green for a reason."

She reached into her top drawer and handed Isabelle a folded-up lily. "Those colors have nothing to do with Nora. They're for you. And what you and only you can do for the fairy godmother world."

Isabelle was surprised to see that Angelica, Fawn, and Clotilda were looking at her in a new way. They were nodding. And smiling. And silently cheering her on.

She finally understood what Clotilda meant by confidence requiring something more. And how fear could sometimes be a good thing. She was also pretty sure she had an important job to do—well, actually, two jobs—and that she was the best fairy godmother (and friend) to get them done.

Chapter Eighteen

A Grand Bargain

The next morning, Isabelle knew exactly what she needed to do first. She had to find her friend, the one godmother who understood loyalty and fairness. Lucky for Isabelle, she was still marching in front of the center, holding her SPARKLY BUT BITTER sign.

Minerva.

When Isabelle arrived, some of the old godmothers stood up. They waved their signs in her face. They had been marching for a long time, and although they weren't ready to give up, they were also really tired.

One shouted, "We're not Worsts." But most of them didn't bother. They could see it was only Isabelle.

"Is your grandmomma coming?" Minerva asked. "Is she finally ready to give in?"

Isabelle waved Minerva away from the picket line, and the old godmother joined her under the gnarly tree.

"While you've been picketing, I've been exploring the regular world," Isabelle said.

Minerva's face drooped and sagged. It looked like she couldn't smile—even if she wanted to. "And?"

"I found out that sparkles don't work on boys."

Minerva chuckled—just a little bit. "That must have been a doozy."

"It wasn't a doozy at all," Isabelle said, conveniently leaving out the part about the bad sparkles. "One sparkle made Mason wreck six soccer balls. Then a couple more made him read mushy poetry and bray like a donkey."

Now Minerva laughed. "When magic is in the air, people do foolish things."

Isabelle agreed. She told Minerva about Nora and the tournament. "She's going to have a terrible birthday unless I get there and help. So I've come to offer you a compromise. I need to help Nora, but I need sparkles to do it. You want Grandmomma to listen. I can help you get what you want."

Minerva reminded Isabelle that the trainees' troubles had begun when she refused to perform her Level Two assignment. (She couldn't hurt her Level One princess.) "If you break the rules," she said, "your grandmomma will blame me, and the word *WAR* will be the least of our problems."

Isabelle agreed. "I promise I won't grant any wishes. I'll only use your sparkles to travel. I won't even tell her who I am. But I can't abandon her. It just isn't fair. I thought you of all people would understand."

Of course, Minerva understood. (She also liked Isabelle. And she was tired of striking. She missed her princess, too.)

Minerva dug into her pocket and pulled out a tiny velvet bag. Inside were some vacuum-sealed sparkles. Some pink ones, a few white ones, and a couple of red.

"How did you know I'd have these?" Minerva asked.

"Because you didn't do any magic in Level Two. Plus, you're not exactly a first-timer. I figured you knew a ton about the science of sparkles. And I was right."

It turned out that Minerva liked flattery just as much as Clotilda did. She said, "In fact, not that anyone notices, but I'm better than good. So when they gave us those lousy raw sparkles in Level Two, I transformed them into these beauties—*lickety-split*."

Minerva held the sparkles out of reach. "What do I get if I let you have these?"

"Here's the deal," Isabelle said. "When I return, I'll bring Grandmomma the manifesto. I'll convince her to stop using the term *Worsts*. And I'll make sure she talks to you. Face-to-face."

"And all I have to do is give you some sparkles?" Minerva asked.

"No," Isabelle said, taking a deep breath. "I also need you to promise that you'll change the name."

Minerva crossed her arms over her chest. "You're sure she will listen to you?"

"I'm sure," Isabelle said.

Minerva reluctantly (but good-naturedly) agreed. "Okay. Deal."

Isabelle pocketed the offered sparkles.

Minerva grinned. "Didn't I say you were going to be a great fairy godmother?"

"Didn't I say you were so not the worst?"

Then they shook on it.

Chapter Nineteen

Most of the Way to Happily Ever After

When Isabelle returned to camp, she found Nora sitting on her cot with her head in her hands. At first, she hoped Nora was just enjoying a serious moment, but when she got closer, she could see that her friend was unhappier than ever.

"Happy birthday!" Isabelle said.

Nora fell back on her bed. "Am I glad to see you."

Lickety-split, she told her everything that had happened.

"Well, thanks to Mason, no one cares if I like him or even

like-like him," she said, half smiling. "But now the tournament is on the line. The Red Team is in second place, so they need me to play." A horn sounded in the distance. "I'm pretty sure I need to go to the field now."

Isabelle thought about all the ways she could help Nora. She could wave her wand and make her sneakers powerful. Or make everyone trust Nora. Or make them laugh so hard they wouldn't care about the game at all.

Even though it would be a long shot, she could even try to make every single camper fall asleep. She was pretty sure Minerva's sparkles could do a lot more than the spoiled ones could.

But she also knew that, right now, Nora didn't need any special magic.

"You know what you have to do," Isabelle said. "Go to the field and apologize." She handed Nora a snazzy red pair of sneakers. "Then play your hardest—like a princess."

It is never easy having to admit you were wrong. But waiting to apologize is always harder than apologizing.

"Will you go with me?" Nora asked. "So I don't have to tell them alone? Can I wear the ring for good luck?"

"You don't need a good-luck ring." Isabelle agreed to walk with her to the field. "First let's find Mason. I think he could use a friend, too."

When they arrived at the fields, Nora's team was there. So were the girls in her bunk. Mason was leaning against a tree near the sidelines. He looked like he wished he were invisible.

Nora did not hesitate. She jumped up on the bench and asked everyone in earshot to gather around her. "I'm really sorry I made fun of the tournament. It was wrong. I said it because I was nervous. Because I stink at soccer. But now I see that that doesn't matter. So I'm going to do my best. And I hope you'll forgive me."

It was a simple, heartfelt apology.

(In other words, the best kind.)

The girls in her bunk told Nora to get off the bench. They said, "We're sorry, too!" Then they all embraced, just as

Isabelle had with Angelica and Fawn at the end of Level Two. Except there were more girls. And they didn't have an Extravaganza to attend.

They had a big game.

And everyone—especially Nora—was ready to play.

Like most stories that are destined to end with happily ever after, it went pretty well—but not perfectly.

In the first half of the game, Ella struggled. (Mason blocked every goal she tried to score.)

But in the second half, Ella scored a lot of goals—Mason couldn't stop her.

To Isabelle, it looked like she enjoyed beating him. It also looked like he didn't mind losing to her. In other words, it looked like they liked each other. Or maybe Mason was right. They were all just having fun.

Nora had her moments, too.

Even though she really wasn't great at soccer, she played with gusto and heart—if not a little bit of confidence. When she was out there with her friends, she looked happy. She even managed to score one goal—but for the wrong team.

When it was all over, the Red Team won the game. But they didn't win the tournament. According to Mason, the Blue Team had already racked up too many points from other games. This match had never mattered.

And that meant it was time to celebrate. (Not the tournament. Something more important. And slightly unexpected.)

"Happy birthday," everyone said to Nora.

And then Mason sang. But not on one knee. And he didn't bray once—even though everyone else did.

According to Nora, it was almost the best day ever. Almost as good as the night she was in the play. Almost as good as the time she hiked to the top of her trail.

Isabelle waited for one more memory.

She wanted Nora to remember her. She wanted that to be the magic of the birthday wish. She wanted her birthday to demolish Rule Three C.

But that's not the way birthday wishes worked. Instead, Nora's new friends in the bunk sang to her. They teased her for telling them she liked Mason. And in honor of her, they all grabbed bags and cleaned the entire camp.

While they cleaned, Isabelle asked Nora, "So, do you think you're going to come back to camp?"

"Definitely," Nora said. "What about you?"

"Maybe," Isabelle said.

Then Nora handed her a small package in a bag. "I made them for both of us to match our rings. I wanted to thank you. I don't think I could have been so brave if it weren't for you."

Inside the bag were two friendship bracelets—one for Isabelle and one for Nora. Nora's was covered with red and orange hearts. Isabelle's was the same, but the hearts were green and yellow. "Any time you need a favor, just ask," Nora said.

A favor was like a wish, only better. This felt like a happily ever after of sorts—thanks to Nora.

Chapter Twenty

Minerva v. Grandmomma

When she puffed back to the fairy godmother world, Isabelle had some work to do—and favors of her own to return.

First, she had to talk to Grandmomma. The strike needed to end.

Grandmomma, of course, agreed. She'd also seen everything Isabelle did. And the truth was, she couldn't help getting a little emotional.

"What a girl that Nora is," she said, waving her hand in

front of her eyes (trying not to tear up). "Is that a friendship bracelet on your wrist? How lovely."

"She is a real princess. I'm sure of it." Isabelle had told Nora she'd never take it off. "But right now we don't have time to talk about Nora. We have more important things to do." She handed Grandmomma the manifesto. "You need to read it. All of it. I did, and I promise you, it's not unreasonable."

Grandmomma waved her wand. A swish and a flick later, Minerva appeared. The ancient godmother looked a little rattled—and surprised. (Grandmomma's magical abilities were very strong.)

Plus, Minerva had never been inside Grandmomma's office. Just like Isabelle, she couldn't resist looking around at all the fairy godmother bling—especially the apple. And the shoes. And the spinning wheel.

"You could have warned me you were ready to talk," Minerva said, giving the wheel a whirl.

Grandmomma flicked her wand to stop the spinning.

"Minerva, for once, stop complaining. I want to talk about the manifesto."

Before either of them could start negotiating, Isabelle said, "First, I think Minerva has something to offer." She gave Minerva a very gentle stink eye. "Even if it is an acronym, *W.A.R.* is not a good place to start a discussion."

Minerva looked a little annoyed, but then agreed. "Okay, you're right," she said. "In fact, thanks to Isabelle, we already changed it." She waved her wand over the manifesto. Now, instead of *W.A.R.*, it read *W.A.R.M.*

"What does that stand for?" Isabelle asked.

Minerva shrugged. "Worsts Are Really Magical. Or Warm And Really Motherly. Or something like that."

Now it was Grandmomma's turn. She sat down and read the whole thing three times in complete silence.

(If you don't remember their positions, here they are:

1. Eliminate the terms *Best* and *Worst*.

2. Select princesses randomly.

3. Make retraining feel nicer.

4. Fix the drafts in the castles already!

They really weren't that unreasonable.)

As she read, the grandmother clock ticked loudly and steadily. Grandmomma jotted down some notes. When she was done, the clock chimed.

"I agree that being called a Worst is not very nice," Grandmomma said. "But the Bests like being called the Bests."

"What if we call you the Goods?" Isabelle suggested to Minerva.

Minerva shook her head. "That would be like calling us the Okeydokes. Or the Fines. Or, even worse, the Competents."

Isabelle laughed. She had seen how humor made awkward moments easier. "What about the Good Enoughs?"

Grandmomma smiled. "Or the Not Half Bads?"

"Or what if," Isabelle said, "we simply call all of you the Grands?"

That seemed to please them both. Grandmomma turned to Minerva. "Will that be acceptable? The Bests can remain Bests, but everyone else is Grand?"

Minerva agreed it was a good compromise. "Will you fix the drafts in the castles?"

"Already done," Grandmomma said. "You weren't the only godmothers who found them too chilly."

It turned out that negotiating wasn't that hard when both sides wanted to work together. "Now you have to talk about retraining," Isabelle reminded them. (Though she was hoping Minerva would let go of this demand. She liked having the Worsts—or, rather, the Grands—in the classroom.)

"Don't tell anyone else I told you this, but going back to the center has proven very useful," Minerva admitted. "My skills were getting a bit dated. And now they're not."

Grandmomma thanked her for her honesty. "I bet everyone could benefit from some retraining. It shouldn't feel like punishment." She wrote something down on a piece of paper. "And it would be nice to start committees to consider best practices, and research new sparkle science. Would you like to be on one of those?"

"I'll come to meetings as long as we can start using a lottery for princess selection." Minerva smiled. "And if there are cookies."

Grandmomma waved her wand, and a whole tray of cookies appeared. "It's a deal." After they shook, they ate the blue, purple, and white treats (for loyalty, trust, and honesty). "From now on, if you have a problem, come talk to me. My door is open all the time."

"Thank you," Minerva said. She looked around the office, her gaze lingering longingly at the shelves stuffed with shoes. "Your collection is very impressive."

"You want a pair? I really have to clean up a bit." Grandmomma pointed to a fancy red pair of clogs that had been made in Holland (the home of Minerva's first princess). "I'll trade you. For your extra sparkles. If you're going to stay in retraining, I have to take them now."

Minerva's face fell. "All of them?"

"All of them." Grandmomma held out her hand. "It's not up for negotiation. After what happened in Level Two—and those sparkles that Isabelle, Angelica, and Fawn found—we need to keep track of our entire magical inventory. Do you understand, too, Isabelle?"

"Are you talking about the ring?" Isabelle asked, pulling it out of her pocket. "Because you can have it. It got me into too much trouble already."

"Would you look at that?" Minerva snatched it out of Isabelle's hand. "I haven't seen one of those in a long time— I used to love these."

Isabelle told Grandmomma what happened when Nora put on the ring. "I thought it gave her confidence, but Clotilda told me that rings don't do anything."

"The ring is harmless," Minerva said. "But in my day, we used to put sparkles under the stones."

Grandmomma rolled her eyes. "I remember those rings, too. They made everyone lazy. So silly—wasting sparkles that way."

Minerva shook her head. "But if your princess had a secret, they were very helpful."

Grandmomma disagreed. "If your princess has a secret, you should take your time to figure it out."

Clearly, they were never going to agree on everything. (Just as there were all kinds of princesses, there were all kinds of fairy godmothers.)

"Where did you find it?" Grandmomma asked. "Did you swipe that out of my basement, too?"

By this time, Isabelle had her confession down pat. She was great at apologizing. "I promise the only thing we took from the basement was the box marked DO NOT TOUCH. I found the ring on the girlgoyle's claw." As Minerva handed the ring to Grandmomma, Isabelle said, "I'm sorry I didn't tell you about it. Now I know I should have."

For a moment, Grandmomma looked sad—as if she was thinking of someone far away. (Mom.)

Isabelle had to ask. "Did this ring belong to my mom?"

Grandmomma didn't say yes, but she didn't say no, either. Instead, she snapped her fingers and the ring's stone cracked open like an oyster's shell. Inside were two shriveled-up light-blue sparkles.

"Light blue for friendship," Minerva said. "That's a very powerful ring."

"Actually," Grandmomma said, "it's absolutely useless." She gave the ring (and the sparkles) to Isabelle. "Keep them as a souvenir. They can't make any mischief. Especially when we all get back to training."

Grandmomma raised her wand. It was time to magically alert the fairy godmother world that the strike was over.

Tomorrow, all training activities could resume. Fairy godmothers could once again grant wishes.

"You won't regret this," Minerva said. "The Grands will make you proud."

Grandmomma offered Minerva her hand. "I'm counting on it. But first, how about a little cake?"

Two hours later, Isabelle walked into the giant draft-free parlor of the nearby castle. The room was decked out like a typical princess birthday party. There were balloons and streamers, and everyone had to wear a tiara.

Minerva sat at the head table with Grandmomma, but she still looked a little grumpy.

"What's the matter now?" Isabelle asked.

"It's these shoes," she said. "They're hard on my knees!" She laughed. "Also, I ate too much cake. Did you try it? It's very delicious."

Isabelle walked over to the buffet and took an extra-big slice of the chocolaty tower of goodness. There was also vanilla cake. And strawberry shortcake. And something that looked like a combination of all three.

When everyone was seated, Grandmomma made her speech. "Dear trainees, Bests, and Grands: In the fairy godmother world, we should never overlook ways to make our system stronger. So today, I want to thank the Grands as well as our youngest class of trainees . . . for proving that persistence works. And that friendship is magical. And that doing the right thing is sometimes hard, but absolutely necessary.

"In other words, everyone can relax. No one is in trouble. In fact, after careful consideration, we think you learned so much during your little escapade that we can combine Levels Three and Four for your final training session."

MaryEllen and Irene stood up and cheered. "We're sparkly and we'll never be bitter again," they chanted in unison.

Grandmomma nodded to both of them. "Also, I want to remind everyone here of the new rules: If you need a new assignment, you must put your name in the brand-new magic bowl at the front of the room. When we're ready, we'll draw names. In the meantime, eat up! Have fun! Let's play some party games!"

The godmothers enjoyed games like Pin the Kiss on the Frog. They did the limbo and the chicken dance more times than anyone could count. They all joined in for a loud rendition of "Happy Birthday" to Nora. Even though she wasn't there to hear them, Isabelle thought this was an extra-special touch.

So did Angelica and Fawn. "We did it," they said. "We didn't get rusty! And we didn't get in trouble, either!"

Clotilda told them to settle down. "If I were in charge, you would have gotten in a heap of trouble. But I admire your creativity. When you're done with training, you are all going to be top-notch godmothers."

The trainees asked her if she was giving up on Roxanne—for an easier princess. "Never," Clotilda said. "Instead, I'm going to let her take her time and figure out what she really wants. She's complicated, but she's ambitious. That might make her the best princess ever. It also means Kaminari better not get used to being Number Three."

Kaminari heard that. "Oh, you think so?"

When they had all eaten another piece of cake, they took turns trying on Isabelle's ring. When Angelica tried it on, it was red. For Fawn, it was blue. When they gave it back to Isabelle, it turned green again. (No more yellow.)

Luciana and Raine debated whether the time hadn't come to put tools like rings back into use. Luciana told the trainees, "As you will find out soon, believing in magic is an important part of helping a princess make the right wish."

Isabelle liked the sound of that. She wanted to ask them more, but the Bests didn't feel like lecturing. Sometimes, like all fairy godmothers (and princesses), they just wanted to have fun.

Chapter Twenty-One

Something Extra Magical

When it was way past the magic hour and Isabelle was done playing party games, she skipped all the way to the cozy spot between the girlgoyles. Even though she was exhausted, she wanted to tell them every detail. Plus, she wanted to wish on her star. It was that kind of night. The air was thick with magic.

Isabelle couldn't hide it—she was feeling really proud of herself. She was going to become a great fairy godmother.

"Sparkle on," she called to her favorite star. Then she closed her eyes and made her wish. It was the wish she always made to that star, the one she'd made so many times before, the one that came from deep in her heart. But tonight, for the first time, she wished for her mother with gusto. And kindness. And she believed in her heart that her wish could come true.

Soon.

Next, she took out the shriveled-up sparkles and gave one to the girlgoyle on the left, and one to the girlgoyle on the right.

They fit perfectly in the spaces between their paws. It was almost like they belonged there all this time. She said, "Thanks for always believing in me." (She wasn't feeling just confident. She was feeling sappy, too.)

She twirled on her toes and waved to her star. It was late—time to go inside.

As she did, she thought she heard something. It sounded like hello. Or, rather, *bonjour.* (That was hello in French.)

But that was silly. Stars (even the most sparkly ones) didn't speak. They didn't say "Attention" or *"Reviens"* ("Come back") or "For pity's sake, Isabelle, look over here." This was just her imagination—or her love of happy endings. Or maybe this was the problem of going to bed with too much confidence.

But what Isabelle didn't realize was she hadn't heard a star.

She'd heard someone a whole lot closer.

Actually, two someones.

As Isabelle went inside and descended the stairs, the girlgoyles stretched their wings and their jaws and their necks and their claws. It felt good to walk around that cozy spot.

The one on the left said, "Hey there, Francoise!"

And the girlgoyle on the right said, "Good evening, Bernadette!"

Then they high-fived. They did the bump. (Even though things hadn't gone as planned, they'd waited a long time for this moment. Three whole books!)

They also knew they had to get Isabelle back. They didn't have much time. Those sparkles were weak. They were practically all out of juice.

Together they shouted *"Bonjour"* and *"Par ici"* ("Over here") and even *"Reveillez-vous"* ("Wake up").

When Isabelle didn't appear, they put their heads together. They were desperate! (Before too long, they'd be statues again.) "We need to make more noise. And maybe something she can see." They knew Isabelle was easily distracted. "Something even she can't overlook."

(They might be rock, but they didn't enjoy waiting either.)

There was one thing they could do. They warmed up their shoulders and then, on the count of three, hurled those blue sparkles into the stars.

As the swirls of blue, red, yellow, and green flashed

across the sky, Isabelle ran to her window. So she sort of got the message. But she didn't return to the girlgoyles. She thought Grandmomma had made this special fireworks show, all for her. Although this was also a problem with confidence, it wasn't that surprising. A lot of great things had happened! Things like:

a) She helped end the strike!

b) Nora was happy!

c) Isabelle's ring was still green, without a hint of yellow, and most important:

d) She was more than ready to learn the science of sparkles. She also wanted to hear the real story of the unhappy princess. And maybe find Mom. And of course, no surprise—she wanted to see Nora again.

As the colors faded into the night, Isabelle didn't know what she was missing.

But lucky for her, this was not the end of her story. Or her training. (Or even her problems!) Just like fairy godmothers and princesses, when girlgoyles had something important to say, nothing could stop them. That's how it worked with magic. They were all too close to happily ever after to give up now.

Acknowledgments

In *Big Magic*, Elizabeth Gilbert writes about welcoming inspiration and saying yes to new ideas. This series is the product of yes and the power of play—of writing for joy—without expectations or ego. I have loved every second of this process. But I couldn't have done it without the following real-life fairy godmothers:

All the sparkles for my editor Anna Bloom, the amazing team at Scholastic Press, and my agent, Sarah Davies. You make my brain swirl and my heart happy! Thank you for giving me the opportunity to expand and explore Isabelle's story and think about kindness, girl power, magical mischief, the different ways we learn, as well as the science of sparkles.

I am so lucky to never really write alone. Thank you to my many writing friends at home and in all my happy spaces, from the Highlights Foundation, to VCFA, the Mainely writers, and writers.com. I'm so honored to study and explore story with all of you. Every one of you has made me a better writer and person.

Extra chocolate and flowers for the writers that find the glimmers in my messiest work: Jenny Meyerhoff, Brenda Ferber, Carolyn Crimi, Laura Ruby, Tanya Lee Stone, and Elly Swartz. Kathi Appelt: You are the reassuring voice telling me to keep going. And to Lila and Thalia Selch—you crushed it! Your questions really got me thinking!

I have been a protester since kindergarten. To my fellow marchers at the Women's March in Chicago: Thank you for helping me hobble around on my broken ankle. To the man holding the "Sparkly but Bitter" sign: What can I say? You made an impression.

As always, huge thanks to my amazing family of creative risk takers and teachers, doers and makers. I have learned so much navigating this journey with all of you. Extra hugs and kisses for the rest of my tripod: Rebecca Aronson and Elliot Schwarz. No book happens without you. I am so proud of everything you are doing and becoming.

The science in this book came to life with the help of my real life Officer Buckle and husband, Michael Blayney. Thank you for taking your real-world knowledge and showing me (without laughing) how to bring those elements to the fairy godmother world. Also: thank you for always cheering me on. And cleaning up after me. And sometimes, making dinner.

Last, a special shout-out to the many readers who have written to me this year about sharing their sparkle. If we all act like fairy godmothers and godfathers, we can make the world happily ever after. I believe we can do it!

About the Author

Sarah Aronson has always believed in magic—especially when it comes to writing. Her favorite things (in no particular order) include all kinds of snacks (especially chocolate), sparkly accessories, biking along Lake Michigan, and reading all kinds of stories—just not the fine print!

Sarah holds an MFA in Writing for Children and Young Adults from Vermont College of Fine Arts. She lives with her family in Evanston, Illinois.

Find out more at www.saraharonson.com.